Mr. Tall

Also by Tony Earley

Fiction

The Blue Star

Jim the Boy

Here We Are in Paradise

Nonfiction

Somehow Form a Family

Mr. Tall

A Novella and Stories

Tony Earley

Little, Brown and Company
New York Boston London

The characters and events in this book are fictitious. Any similarity to real persons, living or dead, is coincidental and not intended by the author.

Little, Brown and Company
Hachette Book Group
237 Park Avenue, New York, NY 10017
littlebrown.com

First Edition: August 2014

Little, Brown and Company is a division of Hachette Book Group, Inc. The Little, Brown name and logo are trademarks of Hachette Book Group, Inc.

Portions of this book have appeared previously, sometimes in significantly different form or with different titles, in the following publications: *Esquire* (excerpts of "Just Married"); *The New Yorker* ("The Cryptozoologist," "Have You Seen the Stolen Girl?," and an excerpt of the novella "Jack and the Mad Dog"); *The Southern Review* ("Mr. Tall"); *Story* (an excerpt of "Just Married"); *Tin House* ("Yard Art"); and the *Washington Post Magazine* ("Haunted Castles of the Barrier Islands").

ISBN 978-0-316-24612-5
LCCN 2014937379

10 9 8 7 6 5 4 3 2 1

RRD-C

Printed in the United States of America

For the blue house girls

"What luck did ye have this time, Jack?"

"Why, King, I didn't see no unicorn."

Richard Chase,
The Jack Tales

Contents

Haunted Castles of the Barrier Islands

IN OCTOBER DARRYL AND CHERYL drove from Argyle, North Carolina, all the way to Wilmington, nearly eight hours, to surprise their daughter, Misti, who was a freshman at UNCW, on her nineteenth birthday. They found her locked in her dorm room—dressed, but flushed and disheveled—with a scrawny wannabe surfer named Kyle. Kyle wore temporarily indecent board shorts and a T-shirt with "F**K**U" printed across the front. His hair looked casually windblown, an illusion spoiled by the mousse holding it in place. By the time he took hold of Darryl's thumb and said, " 'Sup, dude," Darryl hated him thoroughly. He wanted to yank Kyle's horny, pimpled little heart out of his chest and shake it at him before cramming it down his throat. Instead he said, "Nice asterisks, Slick." (Darryl had randomly selected "Slick" from a list of diminutions that included "Buddy," "Chief," and "Sport.") Kyle blinked and let go of Darryl's thumb. He either didn't know what an asterisk was, or couldn't believe that Misti's dad had just called him "Slick." Misti looked panic-stricken, and tried to catch Kyle's eye. Cheryl touched Darryl's arm and said, "Darryl." Somewhere on the floor a door slammed. Kyle said, "Yo, Mist. I'll check you later," and didn't look again at any of them. Darryl said, "What's your hurry, Chief?" Then they took Misti out to supper.

Along a four-lane strip of car dealerships, big-box stores, and Mexican groceries, Misti picked a seafood place ringed by a moat of empty parking spaces. Its only virtue seemed to be that it was a long way from campus. "Sweetie, I was hoping that maybe we could go someplace nice, on the water," Cheryl said. (She idealized the ocean the way mountain people often do: she said she never got tired of looking at it, but had never looked at it long enough to know if that statement was actually true.)

"You can't get into those places on Friday nights unless you have a reservation," Misti said. "And I gather you didn't make a reservation."

Her phone beeped and she tapped out a long text message while Darryl and Cheryl gnawed on breadsticks and watched. She snapped the phone shut and propped it carefully against the napkin dispenser, where she glanced at it every few seconds.

"Who was that?" Cheryl asked, pleasantly enough, trying to make conversation.

"Oh, that was just my *friend,*" Misti said, almost biting off the *f.* "You know. *Slick.*"

Darryl excused himself and went to the restroom, where he confronted and killed a truculent tidewater cockroach. He thought about leaving the carcass on the floor for the next diner to see, but calling Kyle both "Slick" and "Chief" had depleted his limited reservoir of vindictiveness. So he picked it up with a wad of toilet paper and commended it to the deep.

They had Misti back in her room by eight thirty. She said she was going out for her birthday with her friends and had to get ready. Darryl wanted to ask her just what, exactly, "going out" meant—turning nineteen in North Carolina didn't make you legal to go anyplace Darryl would've considered "out"—but he kept his mouth shut. Back at the hotel, Cheryl halfheartedly suggested they order a dirty movie, but Darryl instead watched a documentary about the haunted castles of Ireland until Cheryl fell asleep beside him on the bed.

The next morning Misti agreed to accompany them to brunch (strip mall, pancakes, no view of the water) but the whole time she glared at them from beneath the tunneled visor of a baseball cap. They wanted to take her somewhere fun for the day (the beach? the aquarium? had she seen the USS *North Carolina* yet?) but she said she had to study for a lab on Monday and then gave them a perfunctory wave from behind the glass doors of her dormitory. Darryl hadn't slept well the night before—he had dreamed he was trapped inside a haunted castle in Ireland—and said he didn't feel like driving all the way back home. Cheryl suggested they head up the coast, take their time, see the Outer Banks. Though both of them had lived in North Carolina all their lives, neither of them had ever been to the Outer Banks. Nags Head was so far away from Argyle and so hard to get to that it might as well have been in Ireland. They sat in the car and looked at a map.

"What do those little red dots mean?" Darryl asked. He needed new bifocals and couldn't read the print.

Cheryl squinted. "Ferries," she said. "They mean you have to take ferries."

Darryl scratched his head. He didn't know anything about ferries.

"Oh, come on, College Boy," Cheryl said. "I'll drive the car onto the damn boats if you don't want to."

Darryl started the engine.

They had barely cleared Wrightsville Beach when Cheryl began to cry. Darryl wanted to cry, too, but he was driving the car. He felt like he had woken up to discover that someone had cut out a vital organ while he slept; inside his chest ached a black wound where his little girl had used to live. Sure, he and Cheryl had suffered when they dropped Misti off at school in August, but that day Misti had clung to them and sobbed and said going to school so far away was a huge mistake, she was so sorry, she didn't want to be a marine biologist anyway and could she *please* go back home with them. They had held her and stroked her hair and whispered, shh, shh, oh Sweetie, don't cry, everything's going to be *fine,* you're going to love it down here, just you wait, you've always been good at science. And even though they had left Misti standing in the dorm parking lot with her hands clamped over her mouth (and they both had fallen apart the second Misti was out of sight) she had still been theirs. Now, suddenly, she wasn't—or at least it felt that way. In her room Misti had looked at Kyle the same way she had looked at Darryl when, as a toddler, she hadn't been able to get toilet training quite right. He and Cheryl had never said one cross word to Misti about the accidents—not even when she smeared poop all the way down the Playland slide at McDonald's—but she had been terrified of disappointing them anyway. Now she didn't want to disappoint *Kyle.* Kyle was 130 pounds of unoriginal persona and indiscriminate sperm cells, and Misti had known him—what—a month? Darryl had loved Misti her whole life.

That day they made it only as far as Morehead City. (Nags Head, they discovered, is hard to get to even when you start in Wilmington.) They turned off the highway and started toward Atlantic Beach to look for a room, but the maze of T-shirt stores and miniature-golf courses and go-kart tracks disheartened them before they reached the ocean. They returned to the highway and checked into a squat, modern, misnamed bunker of a motel called the Swashbuckler's Galleon. Darryl flipped the TV to the haunted castle channel (that night it was England) while Cheryl took a shower. When Cheryl's shower stretched past ten minutes, Darryl knew that she would come out of the bathroom wrapped in a towel, her teeth brushed, her hair smelling of strawberries, expecting him to have sex with her. Sex was how Cheryl dealt with stress and crisis. She said that nothing cleared the fog out of her brain better than a good orgasm. (Not that she thought there was any other kind.) But Darryl didn't want to swab out Cheryl's brain. He resented her expecting him to. He wasn't on call. He didn't do command performances. He had problems of his own. Touching Cheryl was the last thing he wanted to do. In fact, he might never touch her again. A small, unvoiced part of him had always been a little appalled by sex with Cheryl—the low-rent lack of reserve; the hirsute, musky ripeness of her body; the searchlight nipples, the porn-star exhortations and curses. Sometimes she was simply too *much*. All the swashbucklers in the galleon would have been able to hear her when the fog started to break.

Darryl hopped off the bed and hurried down to the deserted pool before she got out of the shower. He sat in a damp deck chair and listened to the filter hum and glumly swatted no-see-ums. Eventually he saw Cheryl pull back the curtain of their room and look around until she spotted him. She was still wearing a towel. Darryl shook his head. Cheryl watched him a moment, then flipped him the bird. He flipped her one back. He gave her time to put on a nightgown and calm down, then went back to the room, which luckily had two beds.

Darryl and Cheryl had met when Darryl started work at the *Argus,* then a somnolent weekly newspaper in a shriveling town. Cheryl set type for the paper, pasted up pages, yelled at the pressmen and carriers, and tenaciously covered the tail end of Mr. Putnam, the paper's owner, editor, and publisher, whom forty-plus years of community journalism had rendered bitter, cynical, and alcoholic. Darryl arrived, fresh out of J-school, having read *All the President's Men* six times, but knowing almost nothing useful. Cheryl, on the other hand, could fix any piece of machinery in the office, and type the court report in less than two hours, and once laid out a twenty-four-page Wednesday-before-Thanksgiving paper while simultaneously arranging to bond one of her brothers out of jail. She had a mouth on her like a pirate's parrot and wantonly called Mr. Putnam "Mr. Puddin'" when nobody else in Argyle would have dared—especially late on Tuesday nights, when Mr. Putnam, down in his cups, was slow finishing his stories. ("Mr. Puddin'!" she would yell from the back shop. "Get your worthless ass back here and bring me some copy!") She called Darryl "College Boy" and treated him like dirt until, as a result of a months-long, near-constant state of panic, he became proficient enough to at least not slow things down. Once Darryl achieved a nominal level of competence, Mr. Putnam drank more and came in less, which left Darryl and Cheryl to put out the *Argus* largely by themselves. During slow times they worked sixty-hour weeks. Other times—say, if the Little League playoffs fell during property reevaluations, or something big caught fire during a murder trial—they hardly ever went home. Darryl drove all over western North Carolina covering high school basketball games, singing "The Star-Spangled Banner" to keep himself awake.

* * *

They of course didn't have reservations for the Cedar Island ferry, and, even though the traffic at the terminal seemed light, the woman selling tickets still made them wait until the last minute in the don't-you-people-know-you're-supposed-to-call-ahead line before she brusquely waved them on board. The deckhands directing traffic weren't glad to see them, either—they obviously didn't think hauling tourists back and forth was an adventure, even if the tourists did—and performed their jobs, Darryl thought, with an attitude falling somewhere between boredom and contempt. Cheryl didn't seem to notice. She was fascinated by the disreputable-looking gang of seagulls flapping along behind the boat. She bought a bag of potato chips to toss to them, an act which, in a matter of seconds, magically summoned seagulls from all over eastern North Carolina.

"You shouldn't do that," Darryl said. "Feed the seagulls."

"Why not?"

"Because they're nasty. They'll mess up the cars."

"So what? It's just bird poop. It'll wash off the next time it rains."

"Well, maybe these people don't want bird poop on their cars."

Cheryl snorted. "Then they don't have enough to worry about." She stared hard at Darryl. "And you don't, either." She ate a few potato chips. "I'm going to the front of the boat," she said.

"Bow," Darryl said.

"No," she said. "*You* bow."

* * *

Darryl had been at the paper maybe a year and a half when, without understanding why, and to some degree against his will, he began to hover in Cheryl's vicinity whenever he was in the office. Probably, he told himself, it was because the only other single female he ever got to talk to was the sixteen-year-old scorekeeper for the Argyle High Lady Scots, and her father was a deputy sheriff. He tried to stay away from Cheryl (she had recently divorced a big-armed heavy-equipment operator named, scarily enough, Donnie Payne), but gradually his resolve disintegrated and he spiraled into a progressively closer orbit. He caught himself trying to smell her shampoo. He tried not to stare at her breasts, but they possessed dark powers and tracked him around the room wherever he went. (Cheryl wore tank tops so tight he could see the flowers embossed in the lace of her brassieres.) She tolerated his hanging around as long as he never, ever laid a finger on her scissors.

Without thinking about it much, they began pasting up single pages in tandem, their arms occasionally touching as they worked. Some nights, the paper done, they stretched out on the maroon shag carpeting in Mr. Putnam's office and drank beer and talked about their families (his father was an Episcopal priest, her brothers grew marijuana in the national forest) until they both dozed off. Late one Tuesday, just as they were about to finish laying out the jump page, Darryl closed his eyes and leaned over and stuck his nose in Cheryl's hair. She stood very still for a moment, then carefully laid her scissors down on the light table. She said, "College Boy, what the hell," and reached up under her tank top and unhooked her bra.

On Ocracoke Island Darryl wondered why anyone had ever thought that settling on such a provisional scrap of land was a good idea. It was beautiful, sure—sea oats and sand dunes, just like the postcards—but in one place he could actually see the ocean on one side of the road and Pamlico Sound on the other. The Lost Colony probably hadn't gotten lost at all; more than likely it just fell in.

Cape Hatteras seemed only marginally more substantial. Darryl knew that as a good North Carolinian he was supposed to experience something resembling patriotism when they visited the lighthouse (the nation's tallest brick lighthouse!) but what he felt mostly was vertigo. He negotiated the spiral staircase without looking particularly ridiculous by staying away from the railing, but once they reached the observation deck—a catwalk, really—he could make himself move only a few terrifying steps away from the door. While they were climbing the stairs, the sun had dimmed behind a thin gray scrim of cloud. Small wraiths of mist hurtled no more than a hundred feet above their heads toward the mainland. Darryl had to keep his back pressed against the wall to avoid being sucked into the void. A bemused park ranger moved over and made room for him.

Cheryl gamely marched up to the rail and faced into the chilly breeze whipping in from the sea. "I never get tired of looking at the ocean," she said.

Darryl turned his head slowly toward the ranger. He didn't want to make any sudden moves. "You must get tired of hearing people say that," he said.

Cheryl shot Darryl a look over her shoulder.

"Nah," the ranger said. "I get tired of people spitting over the side."

While Cheryl gazed stiffly into the distance—proving for Darryl's benefit that she did not, thank you very much, *ever* get tired of looking at the ocean—he studied the half-mile-long track over which the lighthouse had recently been dragged to keep it from toppling into the Atlantic. Someday the ocean would threaten the spot where the lighthouse now stood. Eventually there would be no place left to move it to. They were all going to die and there was nothing they could do about it. Darryl edged back toward the door.

"Weather coming," the ranger said.

"Tell me about it," Darryl said.

Darryl and Cheryl were married in a civil ceremony in South Carolina because the idea of their families mixing at a formal wedding was simply too painful to contemplate. When they came back from their honeymoon in Myrtle Beach, people made fun of them because their names rhymed. Cheryl told them they could kiss her white ass, but she wasn't really mad. Darryl tried to explain to everyone that, well, technically, it was only a close rhyme. The hours they worked at the paper weren't any better, but at least now, late on Tuesdays, they could lock Mr. Putnam's door and clear the fog out of Cheryl's brain. Mr. Putnam, God bless him, left them the paper when his liver gave out. Darryl became editor and publisher; Cheryl promoted herself to production manager.

Real estate boomed in the mountains around Argyle. Florida Yankees moved in by the Town Car load. Golf courses spread like mold through the valleys, and gated communities climbed up the ridges. Argyle grew a bypass, and a Super Wal-Mart sprouted like a toadstool alongside it. Ad revenue skyrocketed. They hired a couple of kids straight out of J-school who didn't know anything useful and took the paper biweekly. They took out a loan that caused muscle spasms in Darryl's neck for the better part of a week. They built a bigger building and bought a new press. Cheryl had a baby. She picked the name Misti Renee and stuffed the baby into a sling and went back to work. They hired another kid from J-school and two more ad salesmen and somehow, miraculously, the *Argus* blossomed into the *Daily Argus.* Misti learned to walk by holding onto the receptionist's desk. She hummed happily underneath the light table. Darryl walked through the building and wondered, who *are* all these people?

They drove into the fog—an honest-to-God, Graveyard of the Atlantic *bank* of fog—just north of Avon. Cheryl rolled down her window. Darryl could hear the surf smashing itself into spray somewhere close by, but he could not see it, a sensation he found unnerving. He imagined a bridge out, a causeway unfinished, a flimsy barricade, the road disappearing into the sea. He wouldn't be able to stop in time. He leaned closer to the windshield. He couldn't see where he was going.

"Roll that window up," he said.

"Nope," Cheryl answered. "I want to hear a foghorn."

When Darryl reached for the master switch on the console, Cheryl stuck her arm out of the car. Darryl bumped the switch a couple of times, nudging her arm with the glass.

"Darryl," she said calmly. "Trust me. You do not want to do that."

Actually, that was exactly what he wanted to do. He wanted to roll Cheryl's arm up in the car window. He wanted to jam the switch forward until it broke. Cheryl reached over with her left hand and placed it on top of his right hand.

"If Misti lets that weasel get in her pants, it's all your fault," he said, surprising himself, knowing as he said it that it was the most unfair thing he had ever said to anyone.

Cheryl lifted his hand off the console and dropped it into his lap. "I don't know what your problem is," she said, "but if you touch that switch one more time I will backhand you in the mouth."

Darryl placed his hand on the steering wheel. He felt a laugh fluttering irrationally inside his chest. Now that he'd gotten this thing rolling, he found that he didn't want to ride it all the way to the bottom. He suddenly wanted to see Cheryl walk out of the bathroom wrapped in a towel. He wanted her nipples to lock him in their transfixing gaze. He took a deep breath.

Cheryl held up her index finger to cut him off. "Right now," she said, "you just need to shut the hell *up.* All I wanted to hear was a foghorn."

Misti was not allowed to touch Cheryl's scissors, either. Misti took gymnastics. Misti took ballet. Misti learned to read by climbing onto the light table and sounding out headlines. Misti joined the swim team, but she didn't like it. Misti grew taller than the other girls in her class. Darryl put up a hoop in the parking lot and he and Misti shot baskets after school. Misti played center for the Lady Scots. She was All-Conference her senior year. Some guys from Ohio offered Darryl and Cheryl three million dollars for the *Argus* and they sold it. Darryl took up fly-fishing, which he wasn't very good at. Cheryl worked part time at a fudge shop owned by her aunt. Darryl and Cheryl drove Misti to Wilmington and left her standing in the parking lot of a dormitory with her hands clamped over her mouth.

They didn't reach Nags Head until after dark and then had trouble finding a room in the fog. Every time Cheryl managed to identify one of the vaporous buildings as a motel, Darryl had already driven past its entrance. "If you don't slow down," she said, "you're going to miss the spooks in Scotland."

Traffic lights swam at them out of nowhere, each as unexpected as a UFO. Darryl had no idea where he was going, only that it wasn't toward Argyle. "About back there . . ." he said.

Cheryl didn't look at him. "I'm about starved," she said. "Keep a lookout for a Hardee's or something."

She would forgive him, just not yet. He was lucky she hadn't knocked his teeth out. That he had kept his teeth all these years when he so obviously didn't deserve them seemed a minor blessing. He kept his hands on the wheel at ten and two and savored the domestic missions of the moment. Find me a Hardee's. Find me a room. Stay with me until I die. It was all the same thing, really.

He had begun to consider turning around for another pass through Nags Head when the words "Wade-n-Sea" materialized in sizzling pink neon high above the roadway to their right.

Cheryl leaned forward and stared up at the sign. "That's got to be a motel," she said.

"Or maybe God needs a copyeditor."

"Just shut up and slow down, Darryl."

He managed to steer the car into the parking lot of an ancient red-brick motel. Three low wings of eight or ten rooms lay moored in the fog in a U around the sign, and beneath the sign glittered a small, dazzlingly bright swimming pool. Three pickup trucks with fishing-rod holders welded to their front bumpers were the only other vehicles in the lot.

When Darryl rang the bell in the office, a desiccated old woman with skin cured the color of nicotine opened the door behind the counter. Through the doorway he saw an even older man slumped in a wheelchair, his mouth agape in what seemed to be a permanent expression of disbelief. The wet light of a muted television wavered on the wall behind him.

The woman studied Darryl's face with the wariness of

someone who had been held up more than once. "That's my husband," she said. "I try to bring him home on weekends."

"Do you have a room available?"

"You saw the parking lot. How many do you want?"

Darryl smiled. "How about one?"

"King or double?"

He chewed on his upper lip, considering the ways the evening might go. "Double, I guess."

"That'll be eighty-five for the night. Who's the other bed for?"

"My wife. She's in the car."

The old woman pushed a registration slip toward him. "Well, enjoy it while you can."

"Excuse me?"

"The Wade-n-Sea. This might be the winter the nor'easters finally finish us off. The next time we close her down, she might not open up again. New moon, we already get water up in the front rooms. Can't rent 'em anymore."

"Will you rebuild?"

"Nah. The beach is gone. Government says whatever falls in the ocean on this side of the road stays in the ocean. I guess we'll take their money. Let 'em have it. Move to Burlington. We got a daughter there. You ever been to Burlington?"

"I've passed by it on the interstate."

"Well, it ain't much of a place if you ask me. Shit. Computer's down again. Don't know why we even got a computer. Pay me tomorrow." She placed a key on top of Darryl's credit card and slid the card across the counter. "Number four, two doors down, this side. No smoking. No parties. No loud music. No unregistered guests. No glass bottles by the pool. No exceptions."

"Yes, ma'am."

"I smoke in here, but it's my motel, so don't even bother complaining to me about that."

"I won't," Darryl said. "I promise." He turned toward the door.

"So what are you going to do?" the old woman asked.

Darryl frowned. "About what?"

"Tomorrow. While you're here."

"Oh," he said. "I don't know. Wright Brothers Memorial, I guess. The beach if the fog clears out. I don't know what else there is."

The old woman put her hands on the counter and leaned toward him. "Jockey Ridge," she said. "Now, that's a thing worth seeing."

"What's Jockey Ridge?"

"Sand dunes. Big as mountains. You climb to the top and run down 'em. *Whee.*"

"Thank you. We'll take a look."

"Check-out time's eleven, but go ahead and sleep late if you want. What the hell. Soon as we sell this place I'm gonna sleep a long time."

The walls of their room were paneled in knotty pine, but the wood had darkened so much over the years that it absorbed most of the light emitted by the forty-watt bulbs in the lamps.

The green carpet smelled vaguely of mildew overlaid with mothballs. The pink tile and fixtures in the bathroom looked original, but the toilet didn't flush properly. At least everything seemed reasonably clean.

"Which bed do you want?" Cheryl asked.

Darryl waited to see if she was joking, then pointed at the one by the window. The blinds glowed softly with diffuse pink light.

Cheryl plopped onto the other bed and reached for the remote. "Sorry, Slick. No haunted castles tonight."

"But it's *Scot*land."

She turned on the television. "Boo," she said. "How's that?"

When he started awake, he heard the shower running. It was after midnight. On television the haunted-castle psychic, wearing a headlamp, stooped through a low doorway followed by the haunted-castle cynic, an attractive but bitter little woman in a black turtleneck.

Darryl smiled.

"Do you feel that, Shelia?" the psychic asked. "That cold air. My God, the temperature's plummeting like a stone. Do you feel it?"

"How do you know it's not a draft?" Shelia asked, wrapping her arms around herself. "I don't think castles are insulated very well."

The psychic strode farther into the room. "William?" he called out. "William, are you here with us? Can you make a sound, William? We mean you no harm."

When the water stopped running in the bathroom, Darryl hopped up and found the remote and turned off the television. He took off his shirt and T-shirt, then his pants. He looked at himself in the mirror, then put his T-shirt back on. He lay down on Cheryl's bed and propped his hands behind his head.

When Cheryl came out of the bathroom, she was wearing sweatpants and socks and the long T-shirt she normally wore over her swimsuit. Her eyes were dangerously bloodshot.

Darryl swung his legs off the bed and reached for his pants.

"I can't believe what you said to me," Cheryl said. "Nobody's ever said anything like that to me before, not ever."

"I'm sorry," Darryl said, looking desperately around for his shoes. "I tried to apologize but you just wanted me to find you a Hardee's."

"You think just because I lived in a trailer for a year and a half I'm a slut?"

"What?"

"You think Misti's gonna screw every boy in Wilmington because I like to go to Gatlinburg to see the Christmas lights?"

"I don't know what the hell you're talking about," Darryl said. "What *are* you talking about?"

"You do, too, know what I'm talking about. You think because I like to, what else, listen to the race on the radio, that I don't have any morals."

"I didn't say that. I didn't say anything like that. Do you know where I put my shoes?"

"That's exactly what you said. Well, let me tell you something. The race is a hell of a lot better than that classical PBS shit you pretend you like and make everybody else listen to, and I've only had sex with two people in my whole life and I married both of them so you can just stick your shoes up your Carolina-blue Episcopal ass."

"Cheryl, you're not making any sense, and, for the record, you don't have to bring Donnie into this."

"Don't you dare tell me I'm not making any sense, and, for the *record*, I'll talk about Donnie Payne if I want to. I know you think I'm stupid. I know you think my armpits smell bad and my boobs are too big. I know you laugh at my clothes behind my back. You always have."

"I have never laughed at your clothes."

"Liar. You think I don't know why you give me all that preppy L.L. Bean crap for my birthday? And you want to hear about Donnie Payne? I'll tell you about Donnie Payne. Donnie Payne *liked* my clothes and Donnie Payne *liked* the way I smelled and Donnie Payne flat-out *loved* my boobs, and if Donnie Payne hadn't got drunk and run around on me with Carmen Skipper I'd still be married to him. I wouldn't have pissed on you if you'd been on fire."

"Cheryl, don't say that."

"And I'd have been better off, too. You've been looking down on me from the moment you walked out of Mr. Putnam's office in that stupid necktie and I'm done with it. I've never done anything but bust my ass my whole life and I've tried to be a good mama to Misti since the day she was born and look how it's all turning out. It ain't fair, none of it. So, fuck you."

The Wade-n-Sea sign was so tall that from the parking lot Darryl couldn't even see the letters. The steel stalk simply seemed to disappear into an electrical pink cloud. Darryl thought briefly about climbing it. Out of sight overhead the neon spat and hummed.

On the far side of the swimming pool the old woman waved a long-handled skimmer through the water, while beside her the old man slouched in his wheelchair. Occasionally he lifted an arm and pointed. Despite the blue light shimmering upward from the water, the fog rendered their forms incorporeal. Darryl tiptoed carefully across the parking lot toward the pool, bent slightly at the waist, staring at the ground. He didn't have on his glasses and didn't want to step on anything that would hurt his bare feet. He hadn't been able to find one of his shoes.

"Everything all right in there?" the old woman asked.

"Ma'am?"

"The room. Everything all right with the room?" She pulled the skimmer out of the pool and tapped the mesh twice against the white gravel behind her just off the walkway. Dead and dying moths, maybe hundreds of them, bobbed and fluttered on the surface of the water.

"Oh, yes, ma'am," Darryl said. "The room's fine. Except maybe the toilet. The toilet doesn't flush very well."

"Not enough fall," the old woman said. "It was like that

when we opened the place in fifty-one. Nothing to be done. I got a plunger you can use."

"We're good for now, I think," Darryl said, reflexively touching his back pocket. He had stopped carrying a reporter's notebook when they sold the paper, but still tended to classify people according to whether he thought he could get a feature out of them. Old people were good bets because, even if they had nothing else to say, you could still get most of them to talk about the way things used to be. Old guys at fruit stands had been his secret weapon against slow news days.

Darryl pointed up into the fog. "Tell me about your sign," he said.

"It's grandfathered in," she said, "if that's what you're wondering about. You can't build them that high anymore. People have told me they've seen it from three miles out, but that's probably bullshit. I never went to look."

The old man raised his arm.

"That one?" she asked, dipping a moth out of the water. "Oh, look at that. That's a big bastard." She tapped the moth out on the gravel. "A few years ago some nice gay fellows tried to get it declared a national historic something-or-other, but nothing ever came of it. I think they liked it because it was pink."

Darryl touched his back pocket again. He didn't have a newspaper to write for, or even a notebook to write in, but decided to go ahead and interview them anyway. He thought he'd been tired of the newspaper business when they sold the *Argus*—all those sordid AP stories about Clinton's sexual predilections, or the feature one of his young reporters brought him about an "authentic mountain dulcimer player" who actually had an MBA from the University of Miami—but now he knew better.

"Of course, the amazing thing about that sign," the old woman continued, "is that none of the hurricanes ever broke the neon. We've never had to replace a single tube. We've replaced the roof four times and we've been flooded more times than I can count, but the damn glass never broke. We've been on several news shows about it."

"That is amazing."

"The gay fellows thought so. They have a bed and breakfast up the road in Kitty Hawk. It looks like a nice enough place, but I've never gone inside. We tried a continental breakfast for a while, but it was a pain in the ass. Every morning people cleaned us out and took all the food back to their rooms, even those tiny little boxes of cereal, so we said screw it."

The old man slapped his hand once against the arm of his wheelchair, then pointed at the water. The old woman turned toward him and put her free hand on her hip before looking again at Darryl.

"Tell me something," she said. "Are you planning on swimming in this pool tomorrow?"

"No, ma'am, I don't think so."

"Then the hell with it. I'm not going to worry about it anymore." She dropped the skimmer onto the sidewalk and turned to face the old man. "I said I'm not going to worry about it anymore." She turned back to Darryl and pointed at two deck chairs. "You want to sit down?"

"Sure."

"Jorge should've had the cover on by now, but he's a lazy prick."

"Jorge?"

"Well, I shouldn't have said that. He's not really a lazy prick, I don't guess. He's married to Dolores. He works full time at the Holiday Inn and just moonlights over here. He still needs to get his ass over here and put the cover on, though. Remind me to get on Dolores about it tomorrow."

The old man slowly raised his head and mumbled something.

"Listen at that. This one over here doesn't like Mexicans. He thinks they're taking over the world. Of course, I don't know if you've heard, but Nags Head is running out of Mexicans. I don't know where they all went. Some of the big places have started shipping in Russians. The Russians, though, will steal anything that ain't tied down."

"Are you both from here?" Darryl asked.

"He's from Florida," she said. "I grew up near Salvo. My granddad had a fishing pier. It's not there anymore. The Ash Wednesday storm took it off in sixty-two."

"How did you meet?"

"He was in the Coast Guard during the war and it was his job to ride up and down the beach on a horse. The U-boats were bad, especially in forty-two, everything was blacked out—if you lit a lantern to go to the outhouse somebody would arrest you—and at night we used to sit in the dark on the end of Granddad's pier and watch the ships blow up. You'd see the flashes off in the distance, and then three or four seconds later you'd hear, boom, boom. Boom, boom, boom. Next day we'd go up and down the beach to see what had washed up and this guy, him and his buddies would ride up and down on their horses and look it over and tell us whether or not we could keep it."

"What was the best thing you ever found?"

"Spam. Oh my God, we thought that was a treasure."

"Did any bodies ever wash up?"

"Oh, yes. That's how we met," the old woman said. "Isn't that right?"

The old man grunted.

"Listen to him. He's still pissed off at the Germans. He's a Jew, so I guess he's got a point. I'm not a Jew, but his people weren't observant, so when we got married it didn't matter. I say if a German's check don't bounce, who gives a shit? What were we talking about?"

"How you met."

"Oh, yeah. Dead bodies. So, anyway, one day I was on the beach with my little sister, probably hoping we'd find some more Spam, and we saw a body bobbing around out in the surf. Naked and that dead white, I don't know if you've ever seen that color. The fish and crabs had been at it, but we'd grown up around a pier and seen stuff like that. So we just squatted down and watched it because we didn't have anything else to do. You couldn't tell if it was German or American."

She tilted her head at the old man.

"Just then he rode up on his horse, all handsome in his Smokey the Bear hat and told us to stay with the body until he got back. Well, pretty soon the tide started coming in and the body started to float away. I didn't want him to be mad at me when he got back, because I thought he was good-looking, so I waded in and grabbed it by the ankle, and every time a wave lifted it up I pulled it toward the beach. Eventually I got it far enough up on the sand that it wouldn't wash away. My sister just sat on her ass the whole time and didn't help me one bit. You couldn't make her touch a dead body, but she would gut a shark and not think anything of it. Now she lives in Phoenix."

"How old were you?"

"Fourteen," she said. "He came back with his buddies and a truck and talked to me and found out where I lived, and we started sneaking around together. I'd climb out the window. My folks didn't like it, but you put a teenage girl on an island with a bunch of Coast Guards and what do you think is going to happen? He said he would come back after the war and marry me, though, and he did. I'll give him that. His people had a motel in St. Petersburg, a big pink monstrosity called the Del Moroccan, and when we got married they set us up. He wanted to get out of Florida, be his own man, and I never really wanted to live on the mainland, so we came back to Nags Head. There wasn't much here then. We were the only brick motel on the island. The tall sign was his idea. I thought up Wade-n-Sea."

The old man snorted through his nose.

"He wanted to call the place the Del Conquistador," she

said, "but I thought it sounded like somebody's name. Hey, look, everybody. It's Dale Conquistador. We were busy as we could be for a long time. Filled up all season. The same people came back every year. They would have kids and then their kids would grow up and have kids and the roof would blow off and we would put it back on and everybody would come back the next year."

"It sounds like you've had a nice life," Darryl said.

"You hear that?" the old woman said. "He says it sounds like we've had a nice life."

The old man waved as if swatting away a slow-moving mosquito.

"This one here," she said, "he always had to have a new Cadillac, and he always had to have a fast boat, and he always had to have some little waitress tramp of a girlfriend, and in the winter when we went to Florida he had to be a big shot at the track, throwing money around, leaving big tips."

The old man raised his chin and gazed levelly at the old woman. Darryl couldn't read his expression.

"Big, shiny Cadillacs," the old woman said, shaking her head. "He hates a Japanese car as bad as he hates a German. He thinks the Japanese are in cahoots with the Mexicans. Oh, and the Chinese. They're in on it now. Is your car Japanese?"

"Swedish," Darryl said.

"You hear that? He says that car is Swedish."

The old man lowered his head.

Darryl leaned toward the old woman. "If you don't mind my asking," he said, "how did you two stay together?"

The old woman blinked at him and twisted slightly in her chair. He had asked the question he shouldn't have asked until the end of the interview. He was losing his touch.

"That's kind of a personal question," she said. "What's the matter? You and your wife not getting along?"

"No, ma'am. Not really."

"Well, since you're so damn curious, let me tell you the secret to a long marriage. If you want to stay together, then don't leave."

"That's it?"

"That's it."

The old man nodded.

She put her hands on her knees and stood up. "You hear that?" she said to him. "Tide's almost in."

Darryl hadn't noticed the boom and shush of the surf until the old woman mentioned it. He wondered how that was possible. He turned and looked toward the wing of rooms barely visible between the parking lot and the ocean. "Wow," he said. "That sounds close."

"It is close," she said. "We've lost four hundred feet of beach since we built the place. In the early years, when the tide was out it took forever to walk to the water. And now," she said. "Well, now it's time for me and him to go inside and turn off all these damn lights."

When Darryl walked by the wheelchair, the old man grabbed him by the wrist.

"Your car," the old man rasped, "is shit."

★ ★ ★

Darryl was sitting on the rear bumper of his car when the Wade-n-Sea sign blinked off, followed seconds later by the pool lights. The wing on the other side of the parking lot vanished into the fog, save for the indeterminate yellow glow of what Darryl knew to be the safety lights underneath the covered walkway. The darkened rooms fronting the sea disappeared entirely. Darryl walked around the car and placed his hand on the doorknob to their room, but he couldn't make himself go inside.

He followed the safety lights from his wing to the abandoned wing and then felt his way from door to door until he found the breezeway to the beach. He dragged his fingers along the rough brick wall of the tunnel as he moved unsteadily toward the pitch-black roar of the surf. When the wall ran out he stepped off the concrete walkway and pitched forward into the air. Before he had time to yell he landed face-first on wet sand and somersaulted onto his back. The warm froth of a dying wave immediately gurgled around him. He leapt to his feet and jerked his cell phone out of his pocket and held it over his head. It wasn't until the next wave slid up over his ankles that he lowered his arm. His neck hurt and his face felt scraped up. He placed his hand on his chest and checked the thrash of his heart for premonitory irregularities. When he opened his phone the illuminated screen seared an afterimage of levitating rectangles onto his retinas. Satisfied that he wasn't dying, Darryl clambered up the four feet of dune he had just tumbled down.

He found himself not at the entrance to the breezeway but at the open door to one of the abandoned units. Sand had spilled several feet through the doorway and Darryl followed it across the threshold and into the room. The air inside was still and sour, its odor a mixture of mold and the pungent smell of fish and mud left behind after a receding tide. The surf sounded as if it were going to break on top of him. He felt a little giddy with fear. He forced himself to take another step. The carpet beneath his bare feet was wet and clammy and gritty. It was the darkest place he had ever been. He leaned into the room and waved his arms around in front of his face. "William?" he whispered. "We mean you no harm."

He opened his phone and held it at arm's length with the screen facing out, as if it were a torch. The room was empty. No beds, no nightstand, no dresser, no round table and matching chairs, no television secured to the wall by a bracket, no folding luggage rack with its ratty webbing—everything had been taken away. He knew that Cheryl had never set foot in this particular room, and never would, but the fact that this room was so similar to the room in which she now slept, or didn't sleep, and that it was ruined and empty suddenly flooded him with despair. He moved to the spot corresponding to the place where Cheryl's bed would be in their room. He flipped the phone shut and sat down on the floor. Once, four hundred feet of white beach had lain between this room and the ocean, and now only a fragile berm of sand separated the room from that same ocean's inexorable lifting up and dragging away. He knew that the nor'easters were coming, if not this winter, then the next. You couldn't blame the ocean, of course; he understood that. The ocean itself possessed no intent, no peacefulness or fury, save that ascribed to it. The problem was that a boy from Florida and a girl from Salvo had chosen to build something in its way.

Darryl and Cheryl had once published a newspaper, and they had once had a little girl, but now the newspaper was gone (although, somehow, a cruel facsimile of it still appeared daily in their paper box, poorly written and riddled with typos) and the little girl had grown into a young woman whose face only two days ago had clouded over with scorn when she opened her door and saw them. Darryl lay back on the dank carpeting. He patted the empty spot on the floor beside him. He had begun to shiver in his wet clothes. "My car," he mumbled, "is shit."

Cheryl's cell phone rang a long time before she answered it.

"Darryl?" she said. Her voice was warm with sleep, mercifully drained of danger. She might throw the other shoe at him once she had had a cup of coffee, but he was in the clear for now.

"Hey," he said.

She yawned, and he heard her sit up in bed. "Where are you?"

"I'm not sure. I fell into the ocean."

"Are you all right?"

"I wish we had our newspaper back," he said.

"I know you do."

"I wish we had our newspaper back and I wish you were pasting up the front page and I wish we had a good picture above the fold and I wish Misti was under the light table."

"We can't do anything about any of that," she said softly. "That's all gone, baby."

"Then what are we going to do, Cheryl? Please tell me, because I honestly don't know."

Cheryl drew in a deep breath, held it a beat, then let it out. He pictured her with her eyes closed, holding a fistful of her hair straight up in the air. When she opened her eyes and let go of her hair, she would be ready to face whatever needed to be faced. He had been married to her for more years than he had been alive before he met her. It was a fearsome mathematics to consider, a number unrolling day by day toward some finite but unfathomable edition. They had gone to print together 4,864 times. They had spent their youths compiling a record already sliding from the realm of the public into the realm of the historical inside a morgue of microfiche drawers in the Argyle library. Their daughter was going away from them in exactly the expected ways. Darryl held himself perfectly still.

"Okay, College Boy," she said finally, "here's what we're going to do. In the morning, we're going to eat a big breakfast. Then we're going to go to Virginia Beach and find us an interstate pointed toward home. After that we'll just have to see. Does that sound good, Darryl? Because right now that's all I've got."

In all the years he had worked with her, Cheryl had never worried about the next paper until it was time to lay it out, and she had never met a deadline she was afraid of. For his part, whenever she yelled, "College Boy, get your worthless ass back here and bring me some copy!" he had always produced, even on the deadest days, copy enough to bring her. It was the only way he knew to make a life, the transfigurative ordering of event into story, something he could not do without Cheryl. What good, after all, is editorial without production? He stood up and turned in the darkness toward where he remembered the door to be.

"That sounds good enough," he said. "Let's run it."

Mr. Tall

ON THE FIRST SATURDAY in January 1932, when she was sixteen years old, Plutina Scroggs married Charlie Shires in her father's house beside the railroad track in Weald, North Carolina. That morning she bathed her mother and wrestled her into a white nightgown trimmed with lace bought specially for the occasion. (A stroke had rendered Mrs. Scroggs mute, bedridden, and, so far as anyone could tell, senseless as a pillow when Plutina was eleven years old.) Both her older sister Henrietta and her father believed Plutina to be betraying them—not necessarily for marrying Charlie Shires but for moving away from Weald, leaving them shorthanded with an invalid to care for—and quietly but pointedly made their displeasure known. Her father refused to speak to Charlie that morning and despite the bitter weather sat alone on the front porch without a coat until the preacher called him in for the ceremony. At the last minute Henrietta decided that their mother couldn't be left alone for the fifteen minutes it would take Charlie and Plutina to say their vows and eat a piece of cake and chose instead to sit at Mrs. Scroggs's bedside, melodramatically stroking her hand.

Before Plutina left she went into her parents' bedroom and kissed her mother, but not Henrietta, good-bye. Henrietta's unforgivably bad manners on what Plutina insisted was the happiest day of her life added yeast to the grievances and recriminations and snits that had bubbled between the sisters for as long as Plutina could remember. Plutina swore to herself that she wouldn't write Henrietta unless Henrietta wrote first.

As Charlie and Plutina were leaving the house, Plutina heard the window of the front room slide open a crack. Out of sight behind the winter curtains Henrietta began to wail. Her father looked at Plutina and said, "I hope you're happy."

"I am," Plutina said, perhaps a little more haughtily than she would have liked, considering the solemn nature of the occasion. At that moment her most troubling secret was that she loved her father more than she loved Charlie Shires.

To Charlie her father said, "All sales are final, son. Don't try bringing her back."

Charlie nodded curtly and said, "Don't come looking for her, neither." Then he picked up her suitcase and they made their way along the duckboards down the muddy street to the train station.

Plutina's father worked for the railroad as a switchman, and she had grown up riding the train (as far as Asheville to the east and Murphy to the west) but she had never before ridden it as a married woman. Charlie took off his coat and placed it between them so that they could hold hands underneath it. She was too embarrassed to look at him for very long at a time, so she stared out the window at the river and the muddy fields and the houses and barns tucked up against the gray mountains. She thought, with some degree of wonder each time the train passed a farmstead, married people live in that house, and married people live in that house, and married people live in that house. She felt as if she had been granted admission into some benevolent, secret society to which almost everyone belonged but of which hardly anyone ever spoke.

The flag wasn't out at Revis so the train didn't stop until Corpening, where it took on coal and water for the long climb to Uptop. Plutina had never thought much of Corpening as a town (as a native of Searcy County she patriotically preferred Weald, which in her opinion had the nicer courthouse) but when she stepped off of the train the shop windows of the town seemed brighter, its sidewalks more crowded, the errands of its inhabitants more urgent than anyplace she had ever been, including Asheville. A taxicab honked at them when they tried to cross the street. Charlie pointed at a brick hotel with a revolving door and grinned and jabbed her in the ribs with his elbow. She shook her head because she honestly didn't know what he meant. (And when he said, "If the train was going to be here awhile me and you could check in," she still didn't know what he meant.) He led her instead to a noisy diner filled with men who kept their hats on inside, where they sat at the counter beneath a blue cloud of cigarette smoke and splurged on a lunch of egg salad sandwiches and fried potatoes and Coca-Cola floats, a meal that Plutina decided was easily the best one she had ever put in her mouth.

They didn't talk much going through the gorge, but then nobody else in the car did, either. Something about the gorge always made people hush. To Plutina's eye the cleft between the mountains west of Corpening had never looked wide enough to contain both the railroad and the thunderous, pitching river that roiled along beside the tracks. Most of the scary stories she knew were set there—tales about robbers and train wrecks and hangings and feuds and Indian war parties and men you encountered walking along the road in the moonlight who vanished as you approached them. Conversation in the car didn't pick up again until the train huffed over the grade at Uptop and started down the other side. Ordinarily the exhilaration she felt on leaving the gorge behind would have set Plutina talking as well, but when her ears popped at the top of the grade she suddenly understood, with the clarity of revelation, that for the first time in her life she would not be turning around in Murphy and heading back to Weald. She had thoroughly and permanently left home.

Much to her surprise, she found that she not only missed Henrietta but felt awful about abandoning her. Truth be told, Henrietta was long-waisted and flat-chested and hard to get along with, and wouldn't have had an easy time finding a husband worth having under the best of circumstances. But now, because Plutina had allowed the only boy ever to chase her to actually catch her, and had bolted without a second thought from underneath their shared responsibilities, Henrietta was pretty much damned to the spinsterhood to which everyone had always feared she was fated—unless of course Mrs. Scroggs drastically picked up the pace of her dying, which, five years into the process didn't seem likely. (Both the Scroggs girls were good cooks and diligent nurses and under their care in the years since her stroke, Mrs. Scroggs had not only stayed alive, but developed the appetite of a baby bird.) As the train descended toward the valley floor—a valley cut by a river whose name she didn't even know—Plutina became convinced that if she traveled one mile farther away from Weald she would start crying and never stop. How could she have left her family behind so callously? Why, if her mother came down with pneumonia and died because Henrietta couldn't turn the poor woman without help then Plutina would not only be a bad sister, she would also be a murderer. She leaned to one side and studied her new husband's reflection in the cinder-ticked window. He looked like a murderer, too. (Or at least a murderer's accomplice.) Oh, Plutina, she thought, closing her eyes, the world on this side of the gorge suddenly too hard and ugly to contemplate, you are a hussy—which is exactly what Henrietta had called her when she announced that she was marrying Charlie Shires and leaving home.

When they arrived at Argyle in the middle of the afternoon, few people were about and the handful of stores and businesses huddled along Main Street already seemed to be closing down for the evening. At that particular moment the deadness of the place suited Plutina fine. Charlie didn't own a car (yet, but he had promised) and she hadn't been looking forward to having strangers see her riding a mule through the middle of town like some common hillbilly. (The roads, Charlie had explained several times, were too bad for him to bring the wagon.) She walked with him to the livery stable where he had boarded the mule the day before. The livery stable also doubled as a Dodge dealership, a fact that gave Plutina the impression, which she never quite got over, that the town of Argyle was a place where things could go either way. Charlie saddled the mule and lifted her onto its broad back, where she primly sat sidesaddle. She tried to look regal and unconcerned as he led her out of town toward the looming mountains, despite the fact that she was terrified of the mule. Her father had always owned a car, and as a town girl she had ridden horseback very little—certainly never anything as big and dangerous-looking as Charlie's beast of a mule. She would've straddled the animal and held on to the saddle horn for dear life but didn't want the first impression she made in Hudgins County to be parading down Main Street with her dress hiked halfway up to her tail and her legs hanging out for everyone to see.

Charlie's people came from the high ridges above Corpening, where the government had recently flushed them from their perches when it bought (or illegally seized, depending on your point of view) most of the land in Donald County for the park, a scattering from which the Shires as a clan never quite regrouped. There weren't many of them to begin with, and when they left Donald they flew every which way. Plutina had spent so little time with Charlie's relations that she couldn't say with any surety whether or not that was a blessing. Charlie had borrowed enough money from an uncle—whom, incidentally, had lit out for Texas before Plutina ever laid eyes on him—to buy eighty-three acres of land and set up housekeeping in the deep mountains ten miles outside of town. (Charlie's property had figured heavily in her calculations as she considered his proposal—calculations she silently adjusted once she understood that the majority of that property approached the vertical in pitch.) She had almost gotten used to riding the mule, and was beginning to sleepily pretend that she and Charlie were Mary and Joseph on the way to Bethlehem, when Charlie climbed on behind her and wrapped the arm not holding her suitcase around her in such a way that his forearm casually but noticeably pressed into her breasts. (Unlike Henrietta, she was not flat-chested.) The forwardness and broad-daylight nature of this affection struck her as a little trashy, but she was glad to have both the warmth he provided as well as someone to keep her from falling off the mule in case she dozed off.

The road away from town climbed up and up and—each time it no longer seemed possible—up some more. She tried to remember the way back to Argyle as they rode along, but was soon lost beyond finding. They weaved in and out and around the ridges the way a child might have found her way through a drawing room packed with adults. More than once they seemed on the verge of dead-ending into the face of a mountain, only to veer at the last minute into some previously hidden pass; in the passes the road picked its way along the courses of narrow white creeks that bounded down from the high country as if fleeing something. Because Weald lay on a riverbank in a wide, fertile valley, the mountains Plutina had grown up knowing stood politely some distance away from where she had viewed them. These new peaks, however, pressed in on her like rude strangers. They seemed haphazardly piled on top of each other, like toys in a box or apples in a bowl, and left little room between them for anything so pleasant as a valley, let alone one with bottomland enough for a farm. She didn't know where Charlie was taking her, but increasingly began to think that it couldn't be anyplace good.

An hour and a half into their journey the road tunneled through a hollow so thick with balsam and rhododendron that they could see neither the sky above their heads nor the rushing stream whose echo hissed in the leaves all around them. Once they climbed out of the hollow Plutina noticed that the woods continued to hiss even though they had moved out of earshot of the creek. It had begun to sleet. The tiny, flat hat that she wore with her wedding suit was mostly ornamental, and within minutes her hair began to freeze. Plutina's hair had never once froze before she married Charlie Shires and set off on a mule into the wilderness, so she pushed his forearm away from her breasts. Back in Weald, Henrietta would be cooking supper, probably chicken. Henrietta was good with chicken. Their father would be reading and rattling the Asheville paper, which came without fail every afternoon on the train. He was more than likely grumbling about Herbert Hoover to anybody who would listen. Now Henrietta was the only possibility. Plutina had always felt a little sorry for President Hoover, but because he was a Republican (an affiliation that could get you shot in Weald on certain days of the year) she had never said so out loud. With the hand she wasn't using to hold on to the mule, she reached up and patted her stiff hair. But honestly, how could the problems of an entire country be the fault of just one moon-faced man? Shouldn't people at least be nice to him because he was trying? Plutina found the state of the world too much to think about with frozen hair, so she decided to go ahead and cry. If Charlie noticed her sobbing he never let on.

Just when she began to consider the possibility that Charlie was taking her off into the mountains to kill her, they rounded a bend and he pointed off to the right and said, "There's our house." It was small and white and occupied the top of a knob that sprouted at the base of App Mountain. Already more than a hundred years old, it had begun life as a dogtrot cabin constructed out of chestnut logs by some pioneer whose name had been forgotten. Later occupants had enclosed the dogtrot and covered the logs outside with weatherboarding and inside with plaster. Charlie would eventually raise the roof of the center pen and add a second story. Miraculously, for a house set so far back in the mountains, it overlooked a narrow but perfectly flat creek valley.

He helped Plutina down off the mule and they ran onto the porch as if they had been caught in a sudden shower only moments before, and were not already soaked through and half frozen. When he picked her up to carry her across the threshold the ice on her coat began to break. He put her down in the dark, largely empty center room and set her suitcase on the floor beside her. "That way's the kitchen," he said, pointing to the left, "and that way's the bedroom. I've got to put the mule up." Then he was gone. He hadn't even lit a lamp. Plutina sat down on top of her suitcase, facing the front door. Although her teeth were chattering, and had been for a while, she couldn't be sure if the rest of her was shivering from the cold or because she was so mad. She made up her mind that when Charlie Shires opened that door again she was going to call him everything but the son of a righteous God and demand that he take her back to Argyle that instant and put her on the next train to Weald. Her daddy would take her in no matter what he had told Charlie.

Luckily, the barn was behind the house and Charlie returned through the back door with a handful of eggs from the chicken coop and set to building a fire in the stove. They would eventually come to laugh about her rude introduction to farm life, and "putting up the mule" even became their euphemism for sex, but Plutina would find nothing funny about the episode for some time to come. In fact, from that day on she counted each of the succession of mules Charlie would own a personal enemy. (During the summers he did spend more waking hours with them than he did with her.) She listened to Charlie banging around in the kitchen for a few minutes before deciding to join him. I'm only going, she told herself, because that's where the fire is.

Plutina awoke early the next morning, before first light, and one by one considered the surprises of the night before. Her nightgown was still pushed above her waist, and Charlie was spooned up against her, which didn't feel that different than Henrietta being spooned up against her, except that she, Plutina, didn't have on any underwear and Charlie was naked as the day he was born and clutching one of her breasts like it was something that would blow up if he dropped it. She moved around slightly, trying to locate and gauge the condition of Charlie's "thing" without waking it up. (She didn't know what else to call it without cussing. He had not referred to it by name. She had once heard her father use the word "tallywhacker," but that sounded like a piece of farm machinery that would chop off your fingers if you got too close to it.) When "interested" (that was Charlie's word for the way it got, "interested," as if it had a mind of its own), Charlie's thing had about the same girth as a good stick, the kind you might pick up in the woods if you needed to kill a copperhead, and was longer, she thought, than was absolutely necessary. He had insisted on prodding her with it the whole time it was "interested," and not just in the place she had expected him to prod her with it, but wherever it happened to be aimed. She had found the constant poking irritating (how would you like it if somebody spent half the night jabbing you with a stick?) but when she tried to move her leg or whatever it was butting up against out of the way, or got mad and pushed against it with her hip, trying to drive it back to its side of the bed, Charlie only took that as encouragement and redoubled the poking and jabbing. (If his thing made him that crazy every time it inflated, what in the world had he done with it before he got married?) She wiggled again. Charlie, in his sleep, shoved his thing up against the back of her thigh, except now it was as harmless and squishy—and very nearly as disgusting—as the chawed-up plug of tobacco Henrietta had years ago double-dared her to step on with one of her bare feet.

The sheets, she figured, and probably her best nightgown, had to be a sight. If it hadn't snowed she was going to find out first light where Charlie kept the washtub, then build a fire and give everything a good scrubbing. (She could only hope they hadn't gotten any blood on the quilts; blood was nearly impossible to get out of a quilt.) As for the sex itself, well, that had hurt worse than she had thought it would—which was saying something, because after Plutina started going out with Charlie Shires, Henrietta had been explicit in her speculation about the pain girls experienced when they lost their virginity. It's like getting shot with a gun. It's like being crucified. It's like getting branded. Henrietta had only been trying to scare her, of course, but her speculations hadn't been that far off the mark. On first consideration, Plutina's "female place" seemed a receptacle entirely ill-suited for its apparently God-ordained purpose. No, Henrietta, it's more like sticking an ax handle in a pencil sharpener. Nor did she like the sound of "female place," even though it had been her mother's term of choice, because it sounded like some fenced-off spot where girls were sent to be punished. Now that the gate was open she needed a new word. "Vagina" sounded nasty and all the other words she knew for it were vulgarities.

Still, awful as the sex had been, she sensed glimmering off in the distance the faint possibility that she might somehow be able to find pleasure of her own in it. The thought troubled her a little. The "loose" girls Plutina had gone to school with—there had been three for sure, maybe four—had been rumored to like doing it and she, or any other respectable girl, wouldn't have been caught dead talking to any of them. Was liking sex the thing that had made those girls bad? She supposed that letting Charlie do it a reasonable amount was part of being a good wife—Plutina meant to be a good wife and besides, it was the only way to make babies—but did liking it turn you into something else? Did it diminish you? Would it cause you to lose favor in the eyes of your husband? Of God? The people you passed on the street? Could you be a faithful, Christian wife and still be loose? Plutina had no idea. She had occasionally sneaked and read parts of Song of Solomon when she was supposed to be memorizing Bible verses for Sunday school, but she hadn't been able to make heads or tails out of it, all that talk about young stags and mountains and spices and pomegranates. (What was a pomegranate, anyway?) She suspected the book was about sex, but there wasn't anybody she could ask. Because of her mother's stroke Plutina had never found out just what, if anything, Mrs. Scroggs would have had to say; the one time she had shown a passage to Henrietta, Henrietta had slapped her face and run into their room and slammed the door.

That afternoon, Plutina sat wrapped up on the back steps and watched Charlie chop wood. He grew so warm with the labor that he took off his coat, then his shirt, before finally wiggling out of the top part of his union suit and letting it dangle down behind him as he worked. His bare skin steamed in the cold. Despite the lingering soreness, Plutina began to feel warm and blurry down there. (Down there. She hated that, too. It made her private parts sound like South Carolina.) When Charlie glanced over at her she blushed so exorbitantly that he grinned. She couldn't look at him just then so she picked at a loose thread on one of her coat buttons until she almost worked the button off the coat. She could feel him watching her. Her nipples puckered up the way they did when she ate a pickle. Female place. Down there. Vagina. South Carolina. She twisted impatiently on the step. Now she knew why babies got mad and cried when they wanted to tell you something. They didn't know the right words. Charlie drove the ax into the chopping block. The echo clapping off the mountainside made her jump.

"What's the matter with you?" he asked.

"Nothing's the matter with me."

"Well, you look like something's the matter with you."

"Well, there ain't." She finally forced herself to glance up at him. Tallywhacker, she thought. Dick. Peter. Charlie. "It's cold out here," she said. "You interested in going inside?"

In the spring of 1935 Charlie took a job working on the new road through the Smokies. They had eaten well enough in the intervening years but made only enough money farming to cover the fertilizer bills. Charlie left home Sunday afternoons after dinner and walked over the mountains to the work camp near Corpening. He walked back home Fridays after he got off, arriving at the farm by 2 AM. (How he made the trip through the dark without a lantern was a mystery to her.) Plutina would have preferred to stay with her family in Weald while Charlie was gone, but the farm work fell to her. That spring and early summer she not only kept up her vegetable garden, but she also fed the animals and hoed and fertilized the cotton and the corn and the watermelons. Most days she had to work from can to can't just to stay close to even with all she had to do. The work seemed to her a hateful thing she chased but never once caught. She just tried to keep it in sight, and in the process developed the mannish calluses of a field hand. (Charlie did the cultivating when he came home on weekends. Sometimes he had to work Sunday mornings to get it all done.) Plutina took Friday afternoons off to straighten up the house so it would be clean when Charlie got home. Before she went to bed she drew enough water from the well to fill the washtub. When Charlie stomped onto the back porch she lit a lamp and went out and sat with him while he bathed. If the night was chilly she lit a fire in the kitchen and boiled a kettle of water to pour into the tub. Charlie always washed himself with his back turned to her but whenever he turned around he was, without fail, interested. His thing pointed at her like a weather vane. They had both thinned down to gristle and skeleton, and when he climbed on top of her each of them complained about the rough hands and boniness of the other.

Before Charlie went to work on the road crew Plutina had never spent a night alone. She had, in fact, spent precious few nights in a bed by herself. She wasn't particularly scared during the daylight hours because she had so much to do, but she suffered through the nights. She was afraid that when word got out that a young girl stayed by herself in the middle of nowhere men from three counties would line up to rape her. Whenever she dozed off their faces peered in the window. Panthers leapt into her bedroom and landed almost silently on the floor. Ghosts of the old settlers creaked through the rooms. Haints formed in the mist that rose from the creek and floated on the night breeze toward the mountainside. Large animals ran through the woods and the leaves said *shhhhhhhhhh.* The katydids and whip-poor-wills chanted *run away run away run away.* The mountain itself leaned over the house and watched her. When it breathed in it sucked the curtains tight against the window frame. Once Charlie learned how frightened she was he brought home a dog that had been hanging around the work camp, but it was a skulky, mistrustful creature that spent most of the two weeks it stayed there cowering under the house. One morning she tossed a biscuit toward it while it wasn't looking and it took off down the road and never came back. She began sleeping with the head of the ax resting on Charlie's pillow. She kept a butcher knife underneath her side of the mattress, its handle poking out where she could grab it. Charlie's shotgun leaned loaded in the corner, but she was almost as afraid of shooting it as she was of the things she imagined coming through the window.

But she stayed. Word surely got out about the Shires girl who spent the week by herself up App Valley, but nobody came to rape her. She never stopped being afraid, but learned to go to sleep anyway. Over time fewer faces appeared at the window and the panthers stopped coming entirely. She missed one period and then she missed another. Charlie had the week of the Fourth of July off and they laid by the crops. She didn't tell him. When he returned to work she found herself facing the prospect of several weeks with relatively little to do. What surprised her most during the lull was how lonely she was. She tried taking naps after dinner to pass the time but the house was too hot, the air too still. She always wound up crying. She sat on the front steps and stared down the road and imagined someone coming around the bend—a neighbor girl her own age who lived just over the hill and had a lot of fun about her and loved to play games and sing and sit beside her and lean close and whisper about the boys she knew. But when that girl never materialized (Plutina knew that in reality nobody at all lived over that hill or that hill or that hill or that hill almost halfway to Argyle) she dragged herself up to milk the cow and feed Charlie's hateful mule. When she tried singing alone she found her voice too loud for the valley, the mountain too close and too big, the echo it shot back at her sharp as a scold. The nearest church was six miles away but they were Holy Roller Jesus jumpers who spoke in unknown tongues. The nearest Baptist church was all the way in town. Sometimes she got mad at the silence and went into the yard and worked up her courage and made herself holler out of spite. One moonlit night she dreamed she saw her mother walking through the vegetable garden and woke up heartbroken because she hadn't come in to talk. Sometimes she waded in the creek and caught crawdads and looked into their uncomprehending foreign faces and let them go.

The only neighbor near enough to be honestly called one was Mr. William Tolliver, who lived a mile or so beyond the Shires at the end of the road, on the only other farm in the valley. (Beyond Tolliver's place the mountains became impassable to anything other than a creature willing to crawl through the laurel straight up and straight down.) Tolliver was known to everyone who knew him or knew about him as Mr. Tall, because, well, he was. At somewhere north of six and a half feet, he had more than a foot on Charlie. Although Mr. Tall's front door lay within an easy stroll of her own, Plutina had never laid eyes on him, or even his farm. Charlie had told her to never walk in that direction, and she hadn't. Mr. Tall was a hermit. All she knew about him she had learned from storekeepers and the women in the churchyard the few times Charlie had taken her to town. (Oh, people always said, a little startled, when she told them that she lived up App Valley, that's out by Mr. Tall's.)

A long time before, Mr. Tall's young wife and baby daughter had drowned in the gorge. The three of them were on the way to Asheville on the train. A tree had fallen across the track, and while Tolliver and the rest of the men tried to move the tree, the women and children got out to walk around. Mrs. Tolliver walked with the baby toward the river. The baby fell in and Mrs. Tolliver went in after her. The rapids washed both of them up under a rock, where they drowned. Mr. Tall was never quite right again. He came to town less and less and eventually stopped coming entirely. Now everybody said he would shoot you if you set foot on his place. Of course, people also said that he had reasons other than not being right for wanting to be left alone. He had an apple orchard that his ancestors had planted when they came to the valley. People said he used the apples to make brandy. Twice a year Third Scott, who ran a mercantile in Argyle, hauled a load of supplies out to Tolliver's and supposedly hauled a load of apple brandy back to town. (Plutina had seen Scott's wagon go by and knew at least the hauling supplies part of the story to be true. The brandy part people only whispered about.) Nobody else ever saw Mr. Tall. All Third Scott would say about him was, if I was you I wouldn't go up in there.

One afternoon Plutina was sitting on the front step staring down the road when, for no reason she could think of, she turned and stared up the road instead. She said, out loud, "Why, Mr. Tall," as if he had walked up behind her on the street to say hello. She couldn't see his place, of course, because a shank of App Mountain ran into the valley between their two farms like a buttress, but she imagined him coming around the foot of the ridge. He was walking. He was riding a horse. He was carrying a gun. He wasn't carrying a gun. He smelled awful because he never bathed. He smelled good because Scott brought him soap and bay rum and he was the kind of hermit who was overly particular and washed himself every day. She imagined what she would do when she saw him. She would run in the house and bolt the door. She would fly up the mountain and hide in the woods. He would chase her. He would go on by. She would say howdy when he drew abreast of the house. He would howdy back, or he would stare straight ahead and pretend he didn't hear her. They would talk about how the garden could use some rain and how the watermelons were getting ripe, or they wouldn't. She began to tap the step with her foot. Mr. Tall was more fun to think about than the neighbor girl she knew would never come. It was almost like having a new friend. (She was getting a little tired of the neighbor girl, anyway; all she ever wanted to talk about was herself.) Soon Plutina's attention settled on the wooded, tapering ridge that blocked her view to the end of the valley. She figured that if she climbed it and looked over the top she might be able to see through to Mr. Tall's farm. She bet the place was overgrown and falling in, the fields waist-deep in briars and hardwood bushes and cedar trees, the roofs of the outbuildings collapsed in on themselves. She reconsidered and put roofs back on the barn and the chicken house. She knew that Mr. Tall kept at least a few animals because some mornings, when the wind blew just right, she could hear his rooster crowing and his cow lowing to be milked, and he had to keep them somewhere. She had never heard a dog bark, though.

Mr. Tall supposedly lived in a big house, a fine house, but Plutina imagined the yard full of trash, where Mr. Tall just opened the door and pitched it out. The windows were covered over with the boxwoods that his wife had planted and he hadn't cut back since she died. Poison oak grew up the outside walls and turned bloody red in the fall. Inside, the house was lamp-lighting dark. It smelled like piss and old man. Mr. Tall stayed drunk all the time. He sat in a horsehair chair in the parlor and watched dust float in the single, scrawny sunbeam that sneaked in past the boxwoods. There was a clock on the mantel but he never wound it. He had dribbled canned soup and tobacco juice down the front of his shirt but he didn't care. Cats jumped in through the windows and ate out of the nasty pans on the stove. Mice nested in the stuffing of the cushions on the love seat. His sheets hadn't been changed in years. Plutina almost made herself gag thinking about the sheets. Upstairs behind a closed door was a room with a crib in it. Mr. Tall never opened that door. Plutina didn't have a crib yet. (She knew she needed to tell Charlie she was having a baby, but for some reason enjoyed the secret, her knowing and his not knowing.) She wondered if it was bad luck to put your baby in a dead baby's crib. Mr. Tall, she imagined asking him, what would you take for that crib upstairs? He looked up miserably from the horsehair chair. He waved his hand. The dust swirled. Go ahead and take it, he said. I don't need it no more. Plutina put her hand over her mouth and giggled. "Lord," she whispered, "Charlie would have a fit if he knew what I was thinking about."

The next day she almost had to crawl through the laurel to get to the top of the ridge, and once there couldn't see a thing. When she made her way down the other side she found her view blocked by a cornfield. She stomped her foot. She didn't know how wide the field was, or how close she would be to Mr. Tall's house when she came out the other side, so she just went home, where she pouted but did not enjoy it because there was nobody there to notice. The day after that she took a deep breath and plowed into the corn. The middles of Mr. Tall's corn rows were cleaner than the middles of her corn rows, which stung her a little, but the stalks themselves didn't seem to be any higher, or the ears any further along. She was as afraid as she had been on any of her first nights alone, but unlike the fear she had experienced then, this new fear somehow felt good around its edges, kind of like a sex feeling. Her heart thrummed almost painfully in her chest, but she had to clamp her hand tightly over her mouth to keep from laughing out loud. She suddenly had to pee and squatted in the middle of the field to keep from wetting herself. She bit on her knuckle and sniggered the whole time. As she approached the end of the corn row she dropped to her hands and knees and crawled the last several yards. When she peeked out she discovered a pasture bisected by a small, muddy branch. A fresh Guernsey cow and a slick black mule cropped at the grass. Beyond the pasture lay a barn and a chicken coop—both as sound as she had imagined they would be—and a pigpen and a corncrib and a smokehouse and a shed covering a wagon and several other small buildings she couldn't identify, all of them upright and square, their roofs intact. Even Mr. Tall's toilet looked solid. Across the farmyard stood a two-story log house, as fine as any in Weald, with long windows and whitewashed window frames and a covered porch wrapping around the three sides she could see. The lower slope of App Mountain swept away from the backyard, and the orchard she had heard about rose in terraced avenues for some distance up the mountainside. The trees were neatly pruned, their limbs drooping and heavy with apples just beginning to color. Plutina dropped back onto her heels and shook her head with wonder. "Oh, Mr. Tall," she whispered. "You have a beautiful farm."

For the next couple of weeks she rushed through her work in the mornings so she could spend at least part of the afternoon peeking out of the corn at Mr. Tall's immaculate farm. (When Charlie came home weekends she now had two secrets she didn't tell him.) The yard of the house, she noted approvingly, was swept clean. Not one piece of stickweed sprouted in the pasture, even along the branch; no morning glories clung to the fence posts. Nothing about the place suggested tragedy or despair or even strangeness. The only remotely odd thing was that in days and days of watching she never once caught sight of Mr. Tall. She might have become worried about him, except that from her hiding place she could tell that in the hours she wasn't watching somebody was milking the cow and slopping the hog and strewing corn to the chickens. One day the orchard rows were empty and the next day bushel baskets were stacked at intervals all the way to the top of the terraces; one day the two bean rows in the garden were thick with beans, and the next the staked-up vines had been stripped. Plutina became exasperated with Mr. Tall, as if he had made a series of appointments with her but failed to keep any of them. She began to doubt she would ever catch a glimpse of him, but did not want to stop her spying just in case he appeared. She memorized every detail of his farm and found that at suppertime she did not want to return to her own, which had started to seem small and scruffy and unprosperous by comparison. (Charlie, too, had started to seem small and scruffy and unprosperous by comparison. She imagined him standing only as high as Mr. Tall's waist.) She began curling up on the sun-warmed dirt at the edge of the field and allowing herself to doze. When the air stirred the corn leaves whispered secrets she could almost make out. Every so often she opened her eyes and sat up and gazed across the pasture and said, "Mr. Tall?" but he was never there.

On the third Monday of her vigil Plutina rose from her hiding place at the edge of the field and in a crouch hurried along the fence toward the mountain. To her left Mr. Tall's house was visible only intermittently between the outbuildings. When she reached the corner of the pasture she looked down the fence row and gauged the distance to the barn, which was maybe fifty yards away. She drew a deep breath, whispered "GO!" and sprinted toward it. The cow raised its head and looked at her as she ran. The mule honked in alarm and trotted halfway across the pasture, its ears and tail erect, shitting as it went. When she reached the barn she tagged it and turned around and raced back to where she had started. She dropped to her knees and watched the house intently. Nothing happened. She couldn't remember ever feeling happier than she did right then. She hadn't felt nearly so exhilarated when she said "I do."

The next day she stopped at the barn with her back pressed to the wall. She stole a look around the corner, then pulled her skirt up over her calves and dashed down through the farmyard from building to building to building toward Mr. Tall's house. The chickens flapped up in a ruckus. The mule brayed and galloped away, this time toward the cornfield. When she reached the smokehouse and stopped, she knew she couldn't be more than thirty or forty yards away from the house. She whispered, "I'm going to tag your house, Mr. Tall," but she couldn't make her legs move. She counted to ten several times but remained rooted in place. Eventually a cold point of courage flared in her chest and rose into her throat, where it popped out of her mouth with a grunt. Then she was off, her right hand extended toward Mr. Tall's house. She had taken no more than five steps when a stocky brown dog with a white face and pale eyes and an immense square head shot from under the back porch and made straight for her, running so hard its belly almost dragged the ground. In a panic she turned and sprinted back the way she had come, but hadn't even cleared the smokehouse when she realized she had no chance of getting away. The dog was almost on her already. She pushed up the latch of the corncrib, jumped inside, and pulled the door closed just as the dog skidded to a stop outside. It barked and snarled and snapped and bit at the corner of the door. With her fingernails she clung to the wire nailed to the inside of the door and struggled to hold it closed. She could see the dog through the slats, and feel its spitty breath on her legs. It leapt up and shoved with its front paws against the building with such force that it landed on its back. Plutina felt the heavy wooden latch outside the door drop back into place with a thunk.

Once the latch fell, the dog stopped lunging, as if locking Plutina inside the corncrib had been its plan all along. It remained posted just outside the door, however, growling almost silently, its head cocked, staring at the point where she had vanished. Every so often it turned its head and barked sharply toward the house. (Mr. Tall! Hey! Mr. Tall! Come out here!) Plutina tried to shush it, but when she did the dog leapt snapping at the door. She backed away and looked around wildly. The slats nailed to the outside would have been easy enough to kick out, but the inside of the crib was a cage of tightly woven wire mesh stapled every few inches to the studs and the floor, even the roof joists, to keep rats from getting into the corn. It was constructed so soundly that the door didn't even have a hole for a latch string. A few bushels of last year's corn lay spilling from the corners, but that was all.

There was nothing she could use to pull up the wire. She could see out, but she couldn't get out. She closed her eyes and whispered, "Oh Jesus, I need Charlie to come get me right this instant."

Behind her a screen door slammed, and she whirled toward the house. Coming down the back steps was the tallest man Plutina had ever laid eyes on. His legs were so long she thought at first they were stilts. He wore overalls of unimaginable length; eight or more inches of wrist poked out from beneath his buttoned shirtsleeves. Mr. Tall. He had a long white beard. He dropped a straw hat onto his longish white hair as he stepped into the yard. She couldn't see his eyes for the shadow of the hat brim. She slowly backed against the wire at the front of the crib, but jumped away when the dog managed to insert its snout between two of the slats near the floor and bite at the wire just behind her ankle. She stood in the middle of the floor and through the slats watched Mr. Tall stride slowly toward her. Hot piss ran down her leg.

"Noggin!" Mr. Tall said in a gruff voice as he approached. "What you got in there?"

Mr. Tall squinted in through the slats and immediately stumbled backward. He slapped his shirtsleeves and the front of his overalls as if yellowjackets were swarming on him. "Good... Who... Shit," he said. When he stopped whacking himself he rapidly shook his head. He cautiously stepped back toward the building and leaned forward to stare in at her.

"Who are you?" he said.

Plutina opened her mouth to speak but found that her

breath had left and taken her name with it. Her own hands waved uselessly around her face.

"I said, 'Who. Are. You?'"

Her face contorted and scrunched. A string of snot swung suddenly from her nose and she wiped it on the back of her arm. "Please don't kill me, Mr. Tall," she managed to say.

"Who are you?"

"I promise I didn't know you had a dog and I didn't mean to get all locked up in your corncrib like this and make you come outside. I promise I didn't. I swear."

Mr. Tall closed his eyes and grabbed hold of his ears. He stomped his foot. "Who are you! Who are you! Who are you!" he said.

"I was just playing a game and yesterday I came out of the corn and ran and tagged your barn and today I didn't know you were home and after I got to the barn again I decided to run down and tag your house but your dog came out from under the porch and—"

He stopped her by raising his hand. "For the love of God in heaven before he calls me home," he said, "will you shut up for one solitary minute and tell me your goddamned name?"

"Scroggs," she said. "I'm Plutina Scroggs."

"Scroggs? There ain't no Scroggs live within thirty miles of here."

"Shires, I meant. Plutina Shires. I used to be named Plutina Scroggs before I got married. My daddy's Parcell Scroggs from over in Weald, he works for the railroad, but then I got married to Charlie Shires three years ago this January and now my name is Plutina Shires. I don't know why I said Scroggs."

"So you live other side of the ridge, then."

"Yes, sir."

"And you came sneaking around over here to steal something because you didn't think I was home and you didn't know I had a dog."

"Oh, no, sir. I was just playing a game because I was lonesome and I've been hiding in the corn to see what you looked like but I didn't never see you and then I decided to tag your house because I didn't know you had a dog."

"You were going to tag my house."

"Yes, sir."

"Because you were playing a game."

"Yes, sir."

"And you're sure you weren't trying to steal something? Because I *got* a dog."

"No, sir."

"And I'll turn him loose on you, too, I don't care if you are a girl, if I catch you trying to carry something off."

"Oh, no, sir," she said. "I'm going to have a baby."

Mr. Tall blinked slowly. "What did you just say?"

"I said I'm going to have a baby. I don't know why I just told you that. I ain't told nobody. I ain't even told Charlie yet. I don't know why I ain't told him but I ain't." She watched him look down at her feet. She looked down at the puddle she was standing in.

"Is that your water broke?" he asked.

"No, sir," she said, suddenly aware of her wet dress clinging to her legs. "I accidentally peed on your floor but if you got a rag somewhere I'll be glad to clean it up."

Mr. Tall took off his hat with his left hand and clapped his right hand onto the top of his head. He closed his eyes. "Good Lord," he said.

"I'm real sorry about the floor. I just think I was afraid of your dog, is all."

He put his hat back on. "How old are you?"

"I'm nineteen."

"And you're sure that ain't your water broke."

"No, sir. I mean, yes, sir. I mean, it's just pee."

Mr. Tall sighed and lifted the latch and opened the door. "Come out of there," he said.

Plutina glanced down at the dog. The dog stared up at her. It had blue eyes, of all things. "Is that dog going to bite me?" she asked.

"Noggin," Mr. Tall said. "Get under the house." The dog instantly turned and trotted around the corner of the crib. "Come out of there," he repeated.

Plutina's legs wobbled as she moved forward. For a second the floor wavered and she thought she might vomit. She tried to hold her dress away from her legs without pulling it up as she stepped down out of the crib.

Mr. Tall walked a few steps away from the crib and turned around in a slow circle, his hands on his hips, as if trying to remember where he had put something. "Son of a bitch," he mumbled.

"Can I please go home now?" she asked.

Mr. Tall looked at her appraisingly. "You don't look too good."

"I'm sorry. I promise I am."

"Come on," Mr. Tall said. He started toward the house.

Plutina followed him unsteadily across the yard, watching the line of shadow underneath the porch. Her legs shook so badly that even if he let her go she didn't think she would be able to make it around the ridge.

"Mr. Tall," she said. "Please stop."

He turned toward her.

"Are you going to sic that dog on me?"

"What the hell kind of question is that?"

"I just need to know if you are, is all. Because if you are I think I'm about to fall down."

"Just come on. Don't worry about the dog." When they reached the porch he pointed at the steps. "You sit there," he said.

Plutina sat down. Mr. Tall climbed past her and disappeared into the house. She smelled awful. She didn't know where the dog was. She didn't know if she would ever see her mama again. She stuck the heels of her palms into her eyes. She heard the screen door open and close and Mr. Tall cross the porch. She felt the steps give as he came down the stairs. She tried to stop crying, but it was too late.

"Drink this," he said, extending a glass toward her.

"I just want to go home," she said.

"Drink it. I churned it this morning."

Plutina had never cared for buttermilk, but figured if she

didn't drink it he would never let her go. The buttermilk was fresh, and it was cool enough, and the glass didn't stink, and she thought she might be able to keep it down if she only took small sips. But then she accidentally imagined a bunch of cats with their heads stuck down inside a milk bucket and felt everything in her stomach rush up into the back of her throat. She closed her eyes and swallowed and waited until the sick feeling slid back toward her stomach.

"Mmm," she said. "This is good."

He nodded. He walked a few feet away and sat down on the edge of the porch. "I'll sit over here," he said. "Till you finish that." He put his hands on his knees and stared out toward the orchard.

Plutina looked down into the glass. She didn't see how in the world she could drink another swallow.

Mr. Tall jumped up so suddenly that he startled her. He hurried up the steps past her and pointed at what looked like the butt end of a metal spike sticking out of one of the logs up high near the door frame.

"I'll bet you ain't never seen anything like that, have you?" he said.

"No, sir," she said. "What is it?"

"Bullet," he answered, his eyebrows raised expectantly.

"Who shot it?" she asked.

Mr. Tall shrugged. "Don't know. Indians, I reckon. Home Guard, maybe. Tories. I just don't know." He stepped close to the wall and squinted up at the bullet. "It's always been here."

"Do you have a cat?" she asked.

"A what?"

"Do you have a cat?"

"Nah. I hate a damn cat."

"I ain't got a cat, neither," she said. "I ain't even got a dog. We had a dog that Charlie brought home but I threw a biscuit at it and it ran away."

"You don't like buttermilk, do you?"

"No, sir."

"Then you want some water?"

"No, sir. Thank you, though."

"That's all I got to drink. Water and buttermilk."

"I'm fine, really."

"I don't care for sweet milk."

"Do I have to finish this?"

"Nah," he said, giving the bullet a last squint. "You best be getting on."

Plutina jumped up. The world tilted suddenly and she discovered that her right cheek was resting on the dirt. She wondered how it got there. Mr. Tall hovered over her, his hands wheeling through the air like swallows.

"Shit," he said. "Damn, damn, damn."

She pushed herself onto her hands and knees, made sure her dress wasn't hiked up, then crawled back to the steps, where she sat down beside the buttermilk glass. "I guess I need to try that again," she said. "I didn't do so good."

"The baby," Mr. Tall sputtered. "Is something the matter with you? You've got to go back to your house right now. Ain't nobody here can take you to town if you need to go."

Plutina started to cry again. "I'm just scared, is all, Mr. Tall. That dog scared me and you scared me and I can't stand buttermilk and I'm embarrassed because I peed on my dress and my legs won't work. If I need to go to town I'll ride Charlie's damn mule and take my own self. As soon as I can walk I'll go back to my house and leave you alone and you won't never see me no more, I can promise you that."

Mr. Tall's mouth opened but he didn't say anything. He stalked away from her without a word and disappeared around the corner of the house. After a few moments Plutina began to worry about the dog and eased two steps closer to the back door. If that dog came out from under the porch she was going inside, no matter what. She would run upstairs to the room with the crib in it and slam the door. Mr. Tall soon reappeared on the other side of the house and kept going, his face bright red, striding rapidly toward the farmyard. Before he reached the corncrib he stopped and pointed an incredibly long finger at her.

"How the hell was I supposed to know you don't like buttermilk? Nobody asked you to come over here."

Plutina didn't know what to say to that, so she didn't say anything.

"That's just what I figured," he said.

He came back a few minutes later leading the black mule, which he positioned parallel to the edge of the porch. He nodded at Plutina.

"Climb on," he said.

Mr. Tall's mule was even bigger than Charlie's mule. She already knew it to be easily spooked. She watched it shiver a fly off of its glossy back. "But my dress is wet," she said. "I don't want to get pee on your mule."

"It's a mule," Mr. Tall said. "He smells like shit anyway."

Mr. Tall dropped Plutina off at her house and led the mule away without saying a word. When she called after him he waved without turning around. She went inside and washed herself and changed her dress. She lay down and closed her eyes and pitched instantly into sleep. When she awoke it was black dark. The cow was hoarse from complaining to be milked and Charlie's mule rhythmically kicked the side of the barn. She could hear the pig snuffling in its empty trough. Plutina lit the lantern and went out and fed the mule and slopped the pig and milked the cow without knowing if it was nine thirty in the evening or the last of the dark before daylight.

When Charlie came home that weekend she didn't tell him about her adventure at Mr. Tall's but she did tell him she was going to have a baby. He was bathing on the porch when she told him, his back to her. Moths drew streaks around the lantern and ticked against the glass; from the mountainside fell the shrill scree of tree frogs. Charlie didn't say anything. She watched his shoulders go up and down once. When he turned around she saw he was only half interested. She couldn't tell if it was going up or coming down. He was smiling a little, but in the lantern light she couldn't read his eyes.

"Well, what do you think about that?" she asked.

"I reckon it was bound to happen, the way me and you go at it."

Going up, she noticed. "I reckon."

"I'm surprised it took this long," he said. "I thought we'd have had half a houseful by now."

Something inside her dried to crust right then. Mr. Tall had been nicer about it while she was locked in his corncrib standing in a puddle of piss. "I'm going inside," she said. Wouldn't nobody be putting up the mule on the Shires place before morning, if then.

That Sunday night, after Charlie went back to Corpening, Plutina found she couldn't stop thinking about Mr. Tall. She lay awake and tried to remember everything he had said to her. He had been mostly kind, she decided—gruffer than her father, but still nicer; worse-tempered than Charlie, but more thoughtful. If Mr. Tall had been her daddy he wouldn't have said to Charlie what her daddy had said about not bringing her back. If he had been her husband he would have had more to say about her being pregnant than what took you so long. As she slid into sleep their conversation extended from what they had actually said to each other into reams of talk about everything under the sun. She told him something extremely important that took her a long time to say, but when she woke up she couldn't remember what it was.

Monday while she worked she wondered why Mr. Tall hadn't jumped in after his wife and baby. She pictured him running down the railroad embankment toward the river. Women on the riverbank were screaming and crying and pointing into the rapids. Maybe he did jump, she thought, he just didn't drown. Maybe somebody stopped him from jumping. Plutina placed herself on the riverbank between Mr. Tall and the water. She wore a long black skirt and a high-collared blouse, a cameo pin—she was a woman in an old photograph. Mr. Tall's eyes were wild as he ran down the hill. He threw down his hat. He was going to jump. She stepped in front of him and wrapped her arms around him at the water's edge. He tottered dangerously at the edge of the rapids. He wanted to go in, although she could see in his eyes he knew there was no use. The river roared at her back and covered them both with spray. If he went in he would take her with him. She would drown underneath the same rock as Mrs. Tall. No, Mr. Tall, no! she shouted into his ear. There's nothing you can do. They're with Jesus now. Eventually she felt his arms wrap around her shoulders. He stumbled back from the river's edge and began to sob. She had saved him. There, there, Mr. Tall, she said. There, there. She helped him back to the train.

A few weeks later she heard a soft footstep on the front porch and ran and jerked open the door, thinking Charlie had quit his job and come home to surprise her. Instead she saw Mr. Tall hurrying across the yard toward the road. Beside the door sat a peck basket of ripe apples.

"Mr. Tall!" she called. "Mr. Tall, wait."

He stopped and turned slowly toward the house.

"Thank you for the apples," she said.

"They're sour," he said. "They're not fit to eat but they cook good." He waved and started to turn away.

"Wait," she said again. "Wait. Do you like pie? Let me make you a pie. Come back tomorrow evening and I'll have an apple pie for you. You can eat it with your supper."

His mouth worked rapidly, trying to make an excuse.

"I won't ask you to come in," she said. "I'll just hand you the pie when you come and you can take it home and eat it. You can leave the pan down in the yard when you're done. You don't even have to wash it. I make a good pie. You like apple pie, don't you?"

Mr. Tall nodded, but he looked miserable.

"Will you come back tomorrow?"

"I..." he said. "We'll see."

Plutina waved. "See you tomorrow," she said, closing the door before he changed his mind.

The next morning at first light she sat on the back porch peeling apples. She wanted to get her baking done before the heat of the day. It was a Wednesday. She had enough sugar to make three pies, but barely enough cinnamon for one. She didn't have a sign of a clove. Mr. Tall's pie would be fair enough, but it wouldn't be her best. The other two would only be adequate. She planned to eat them both herself anyway. If she gave Charlie a piece of apple pie, he would naturally want to know where the apples came from, since they didn't have a tree. Plutina didn't see how she could tell Charlie Mr. Tall gave her the apples, without also telling him about the spying and the dog and having been locked in the corncrib and peeing on the floor and gagging on the buttermilk and Mr. Tall having to carry her home on the mule. And while she didn't want Charlie to know specifically that she had gotten into trouble at Mr. Tall's, she also didn't want him to know about Mr. Tall generally—although she tried to keep that part of her secret pushed out of the way so she didn't have to consider the implications of keeping such a secret from your husband. She simply decided that Mr. Tall was her friend and she would keep him for herself. She was going to make her friend an apple pie—nothing wrong with that, just being neighborly—and she would eat the other two. Nothing wrong with that, either. She was going to have a baby. She ought to be able to eat as many apple pies as she wanted to. She would give the apple peels to the pig and the rest of the apples to the mule. That struck her as a waste—giving perfectly good apples to a mule—but there was nothing she could do about it.

When Mr. Tall stepped onto the porch the next afternoon, Plutina pulled open the door and extended the pie toward him so suddenly that he flinched a little. "Slow down, now," he said.

"Here's your pie," she said. "I didn't have a clove, but I did have a little cinnamon in the kitchen. I hope it's fit to eat."

Mr. Tall took the pie from her and stared down at it a long time. With one hand he touched the bib pocket of his overalls. "What do I owe you?" he asked.

"Mr. Tall," she said. "Don't be silly. You don't owe me a thing."

He looked down at the pie again. "Well, I thank you."

"You're very welcome."

"All right. I best get on, then."

"Don't rush off," she said.

"I got to get back."

"Well, come see us."

He touched the brim of his hat with his finger. Plutina watched him start across the yard. "Mr. Tall," she called after him, feeling as she spoke, yet unable to keep herself from speaking, that she was about to misstep in the dark and fall a long way. "I'm sorry your wife and little baby fell in the river."

Mr. Tall stopped and stiffened in his tracks. His shoulders widened. He stood up straighter. He seemed to grow several inches before he whirled on her. "What did you just say?" he asked.

"Mr. Tall, I—"

"What did you just say?"

"Please don't be mad at me."

"Who the hell do you think you are?"

"I don't think I'm nobody, Mr. Tall, I really don't."

"Don't you ever talk to me like that again."

"I'm sorry, Mr. Tall. I didn't mean to. I just wanted to make you feel better, is all."

He gaped at her. "Feel better?" he said. He stepped toward her. "You want to make me feel better?"

Plutina covered her mouth with her hands.

He closed his eyes and threw the pie toward the house, where it splatted in the yard. "You think I feel better now? Tell me."

"Please stop, Mr. Tall."

He took another step. "Let me look at your titties. How about that?"

"What?"

"You heard me. Show me them ripe little titties you're so proud of. That ought to make me feel better."

"Oh, no, Mr. Tall. Please no."

"You know how long it's been since I even *seen* a titty?"

"Mr. Tall, I think I'm going to be sick."

"I hope you are. I hope you're sick enough to die."

Plutina stepped to the edge of the porch and vomited half an apple pie into the yard. She dropped to her knees and held on to a post while she retched.

"And I hope your baby dies," he said. "I hope it dies before I get back to the house."

Plutina closed her eyes. If he wanted to kill her, well, that would be all right. She had made herself worthy of the curse. She listened to him pant in the yard, and waited for him to tromp toward her. Then she listened to him stride away.

Before she had a chance to start crying a rock thwacked into the wall near the door and clattered onto the porch. Plutina thought, Mr. Tall is throwing rocks at me. She opened her eyes and sat up. Mr. Tall stood near the road, his face gone white as his shirt. His right arm was cocked behind his ear, his fist clutching another stone to throw. He raised his left arm and pointed a long, shaking finger at her. "They didn't fall!" he shouted. "You hear me? They didn't fall!" He chunked the second rock, which sailed all the way over the house.

Plutina climbed to her feet. Mr. Tall had cursed her, and

cursed her baby, and she halfway expected him to come back after while and shoot her, but she did not want him, or anybody, throwing rocks at her. That was just too much. She stomped down the steps and wagged her finger at him. She cried, "You better stop throwing rocks at my house if you know what's good for you!" She cast around for a rock of her own to throw.

"Nobody fell!" he yelled. "She jumped! Do you hear me? She grabbed up that baby and jumped!"

Plutina stopped where she stood. "Oh," she said. "Oh."

Her right hand fluttered upward and lit on her belly. As her eyes filled with tears Mr. Tall grew wavery as a haint.

"Oh, Mr. Tolliver," she said, "I am so sorry."

He stared at her for a moment long enough to hold a lifetime, then nodded once and turned toward the road. She knew even then that she would never speak to him again. She would leave him to his laborious grief; he would never utter her name. As she watched him walk out of sight a worry wakened inside her and buzzed like a fly in a jar.

The Cryptozoologist

FIELDIN WAS UNDER round-the-clock hospice care, and the jagged, liquid rasp of his breathing made it almost impossible for Rose to think about anything other than his vain search for oxygen. Unable to sleep, she put on his old down jacket and stepped onto the back porch, closing the door quietly behind her. It was about two thirty in the morning, the world silvered and silent with frost. The orchard glittered in the harsh light of a near-full moon. The gnarled old apple trees seemed on the verge of movement, as if she had caught them marching in formation toward App Mountain, whose black shoulders sloped suddenly upward just beyond the last row of trees. Had she been in a more peaceful mood, she might have fetched her sketchbook and made notes about the shadows for painting later. Instead, she stared at the mountain and wondered, as she often did, if Wayne Lee Cowan was still alive. Wayne Lee had worked for Rose and Fieldin a few times as a sullen and not particularly industrious day laborer, a fact that chilled Rose every time she thought of it. The previous summer he had set off a bomb outside an abortion clinic in Birmingham, killing eleven people. After the bombing he'd driven back here, parked his truck on a Forest Service fire road and disappeared into these mountains. Nobody, at least nobody who was talking, had laid eyes on him since.

Rose had lived on the farm for twenty-five years, and had stood on this porch and studied this orchard and this mountain countless times. But something about the view tonight puzzled her, although the puzzlement didn't immediately register as such. She actually noticed that her brow was furrowed before she understood why. The moment that the unease she felt formed itself into a conscious thought—Wayne Lee—a figure separated itself from the shadow of one of the trees and strode quickly through the orchard toward the mountain. The figure was large and broad-shouldered, long-armed and stooped. Some kind of silver stripe ran the length of its back. Until it turned to look over its shoulder at her, Rose didn't fully appreciate that the figure not only wasn't Wayne Lee Cowan but wasn't even human.

When she ran back inside to tell the hospice volunteer sitting with Fieldin what she had seen, she found the woman removing the oxygen tube from his nose. As Rose stood in the doorway and stared, thinking, Bigfoot, I just saw Bigfoot, she realized that the house was extraordinarily quiet. Fieldin had stopped breathing.

In 1975, when Rose turned twenty, married Fieldin Kohler, and moved to the farm, Argyle, the nearest town, had seemed to be as close as one could get to the end of the earth and still have access to a grocery store. That was why Fieldin had bought it. He had been Rose's painting teacher at the small state college in Georgia onto whose campus she had wandered after graduating from high school. He was an emaciated praying mantis of a man who stuffed the legs of his paint-spattered chinos into knee-high fringed moccasins. He pulled his thinning gray hair back into a greasy ponytail, and wore vaguely piratical linen blouses whose sleeves billowed when he waved his arms. In class, he paced and chain-smoked while ranting about the soullessness of American art, and routinely offered beer and gas money to any student who would drive to Pennsylvania and *personally* shoot Andrew Wyeth.

Rose's father had been an Air Force intelligence officer who came home each night prohibited by federal law from talking about what he had done during the day. Her mother was a perfectly coiffed and made-up alcoholic with even more stringent standards of secrecy. Rose was an only child and Fieldin was the first adult who ever really told her anything. What he told her, though, was that her breasts alone would have made Gauguin swear off Tahitian maidens forever, and that he would gladly cut off his right hand and never make art again if she would allow him to paint her nude just once.

She went to bed with him during their first "sitting." His apartment was squalid. The only painting in the place was a self-portrait, done in the style of van Gogh, through which Fieldin had stuck his foot during a particularly virulent fit of self-loathing. On the ceiling above his bed he had meticulously copied out a long passage from Rimbaud, in French, and he became almost inconsolable when she told him that she couldn't read it. Later, when he went out to wander the streets alone, weeping with joy over how *ancient* her soul was, she got dressed and cleaned his apartment. By the time she realized that Fieldin had been a caricature when she met him, a by-the-book cutout of the lecherous college professor, they'd been married for years and his health was already beginning to fail. Once he became sick, holding him accountable for seducing the girl she'd been at eighteen—he'd been forty-three—struck her as an unnecessary act of retribution. That girl had found Fieldin Kohler terribly romantic.

She often thought with great tenderness about the administrators and counselors and professors who had taken turns trying to talk her out of leaving school and marrying Fieldin. The truth was that she had enjoyed the desperate quality of their attention. She had felt as if she were standing on a high, narrow ledge while they shouted at her not to jump. Until then, no one had ever cared whether she jumped or not, and she was afraid that if she climbed down off the ledge they would stop noticing her at all. So she jumped. Fieldin stormed into the dean's office and quit in the middle of the fall term of her junior year, two days before the board of trustees was due to fire him. The morning they left for North Carolina, two campus police officers prevented him from entering her dormitory. He stood on the lawn outside her window, pretending to struggle with the cops, and screamed, "What have you fascists done with Rose?" The girls on her hallway silently watched her walk to the elevator. Everything she owned in the world fit into two suitcases and a duffel bag. She might have gone with her parents rather than Fieldin that morning, had her parents shown up. Their anger, however, had hardened into ultimatum, and the ultimatums into silence. Rose and Fieldin stopped for lunch in Spartanburg, South Carolina, and got married while they were there.

They moved into the farmhouse in November, during the last pale, generous days of a prolonged Indian summer. A few yellow leaves still clung to the upper branches of the apple trees, like decorations from a party she had missed. At dusk, deer came down from the mountain and tottered around unsteadily on their hind legs, as if experimenting with a new mode of locomotion, eating from the twisted branches all of the withered apples they could reach. Late at night, raccoons climbed the trees and quarreled over the fruit left behind by the deer. From the bedroom she could hear the losers falling out of the trees and thudding onto the ground.

The house was a disaster. No one had lived in it for years, and when Fieldin carried her across the threshold it had neither indoor plumbing nor electricity. Fieldin told her that the modern world was overrated and that they were going to live closer to the earth, the way the Cherokee had before the white man destroyed their way of life and made them forget who the Great Spirit had intended them to be. He lost patience with living close to the earth, however, as soon as the weather turned cold. The only heat in the place came from an antique woodstove in the kitchen and a fireplace in the front room. The first frigid morning, Fieldin went up the mountain with an ax and came home less than an hour later, without any firewood, crying and cursing, blaming her for having got him into this mess. He dropped the ax at her feet and told her to go and cut wood if she was cold. By sundown she had managed to chop up and drag enough deadfall into the yard to get them through the night, blistering both her hands in the process. The next morning, she took to town the credit card that her father had given her to use in case of emergency and purchased a chainsaw. (Later, when her father received the bill, he canceled the card.)

Their only neighbors were Charlie and Plutina Shires, an older couple of indeterminate age—they might have been sixty or they might have been eighty—whose small farm was the only other place in the valley. Rose had already smelled the wood smoke from their kitchen chimney, and noticed with admiration the carefully corded stacks of wood that Charlie had laid in beside his barn, so on the way home from town she stopped and introduced herself and asked him to show her how to work the chainsaw. Plutina insisted that she come in and eat a late breakfast of cold biscuits and molasses. Plutina's blue eyes were hugely magnified by the thick lenses of her glasses, and she sat and blinked, without saying anything, or missing anything, as Rose told her about Fieldin.

Charlie appeared in the woodlot the next morning, bearing his own saw and pulling a trailer behind his tractor. He was a wizened little man who chewed on the stub of an unlit cigar, forcing his right eye into a perpetual squint. He never said three words when he could get by with two, and wouldn't waste two if he could make his point without speaking. That day, without drawing attention to the fact that he was teaching her, he showed Rose how to notch a tree to make it fall in the direction she wanted, how to keep the chain from binding and bucking, how to trim branches safely by cutting away from her legs, how to stack wood on the trailer so that it wouldn't roll off. On the way back down the hollow, he taught her how to drive the tractor. Because she had been cutting wood in a pair of saddle oxfords, the only remotely warm shoes she owned, the next morning he showed up with a pair of tall green rubber boots that he said were too small for him. The boots were brand-new, but it was the mud he had rubbed on them, in an earnest attempt not to embarrass her, that made her cry.

Charlie managed to keep an eye on their woodpile without seeming to, and took to parking his tractor in their woodlot and walking home over the ridge when he thought the pile was getting low. The only way to get his tractor to their woodlot was to drive it through their yard. He never looked at the house as he drove past, but if Rose was outside he greeted her by lifting his index finger from the steering wheel—which was about as ebullient as she ever knew him to be. If Fieldin was outside, Charlie just stared straight ahead. For his part, Fieldin pretended that the clattering tractor, as well as the old guy perched atop it, was invisible. He spent his days that first winter drinking coffee at the diner in Argyle and reading detective novels at the library. One Saturday morning in February, Charlie drove into the yard with a plow attached to the tractor and asked if she didn't reckon it was time to bust up the garden spot.

Rose knew that Fieldin's family had money. She just didn't know how much *he* had. Afraid that he would soon announce that they had run out of cash and couldn't buy food, she planted an immense garden, with the idea of selling whatever produce they didn't eat. She knew nothing about gardening, of course, so she learned how to do it by helping Plutina and Charlie. She planted the same vegetables they planted, though in larger quantities, and hoed and fertilized and sprayed and dusted exactly as they did. To her great joy and amazement, her garden flourished. When Fieldin had the house wired for electricity, she was able to convince him that it would be in his best interest to buy her the largest chest-model freezer offered in the Sears catalogue.

Spring inched in an uneven line up the mountain and didn't reach the ridgetop until the first week of May. When the weather warmed up for good, Fieldin set up his studio in the loft of the barn. While Rose worked in the garden, she could see him through the loft door, usually smoking and staring at a blank canvas propped on his easel. Occasionally, she'd catch him watching her. Cutting firewood and working in the garden had caused her shoulders to broaden and her waist to shrink. She developed the kind of muscles in her arms and legs that she had previously seen only on the boys who played football in high school. Her normally straight, mostly brown hair curled wildly and lightened in the sun. On the days when she knew that Charlie and Plutina had gone into town and wouldn't be dropping by, she stripped off her overalls—another gift from Charlie—and worked in the garden wearing just her underwear and the green rubber boots.

The single painting of Fieldin's that she hung after he died was a gouache of her hoeing string beans. She occupied only a small portion on the upper right quadrant of the canvas, although the converging lines of the bean rows led the viewer's eye to the spot where she worked. Behind her, the mountain was dotted with the white of blooming dogwoods. In the painting, she wore only the green boots—artistic license, she supposed, and just like Fieldin—but her breasts were discreetly concealed behind her arm. She found the painting hidden in his studio when she went to clean it out.

It was during those first years that Fieldin adopted the Trail of Tears as his great subject. He wore a leather headband and, occasionally, a loincloth over his jeans. The town of Cherokee was less than an hour away, and he began driving there once or twice a week, sometimes staying overnight. He often came home in a foul mood because most of the Cherokee he encountered either wanted nothing to do with him or laughed at him outright. Their derision, however, never lessened his sincere, rather simplistic admiration of them as an oppressed yet spiritual people. He obsessively painted large, melodramatic canvases of weeping Cherokee slogging westward through the snow, watched from barren ridges by faceless white soldiers. The Indians were always marching toward a large stone pyramid that loomed in the distance. Because he couldn't find a gallery in Asheville that would show his paintings, Fieldin doggedly carted them to festivals and county fairs all over western North Carolina without ever managing to sell one—although he did, in a somewhat mysterious act of generosity, give one to Charlie and Plutina. Rose couldn't tell whether their neighbors actually liked the painting, but they hung it in their living room, where it shared the wall above the couch with a print, cut from a calendar, of Jesus praying in the moonlight while a storm raged behind him.

Despite the various privations that came with living in a drafty, fieldmouse-infested, hundred-and-fifty-year-old house with a terminally self-absorbed man, Rose grew to love the farm as she had never before loved a place. (When she was a child, her family had moved from Air Force base to Air Force base, and the only place she had loved was her bed, the dark safe tent of its covers, assembled and disassembled in a series of shabby, interchangeable bedrooms.) Afraid that Fieldin would make fun of her, she secretly began painting small watercolors of the garden and the orchard, the mountain always vigilant in the background. Eventually, she worked up enough courage to take a portfolio of her work to Three Weird Sisters, an art gallery in Argyle that was run by a trio of crewcut lesbians, transplanted from Milwaukee, whose specific domestic arrangement Rose could never figure out. Much to her surprise, not only did the gallery take her on as an artist but her paintings began to sell. Within a few years, they were selling as fast as she could paint them. Soon it seemed that every Florida Yankee who built a big house in the mountains had to have at least one painting by Rose Kohler. The only time Rose ever asked Fieldin what he thought of her art, he shrugged and told her that, while it didn't grab him by the balls, he liked it better than Andrew Wyeth's.

In the end, Fieldin quit painting altogether and took a part-time job in the gallery. He called the weird sisters his harem, and they called him their boy toy. At least once a week, either he threatened to quit over the crappy art they chose to display or they threatened to fire him for condescending to the customers. Whatever disappointment he must have felt at giving up painting, whatever resentment he harbored over Rose's success, he kept to himself, even after the state art museum in Raleigh bought two of her paintings for its permanent collection.

By the time they'd been married for twenty years, Fieldin had somehow become an old man. He spent the last five years of his life angrily wheeling a small tank of oxygen around the gallery, bitching about his emphysema and Abstract Expressionism. Rose was never able to persuade him to give up smoking, but he promised the sisters, under their threat of physical violence, that he would at least shut down the tank before he lit up. The slow process of dying never really softened Fieldin, the way it did people you saw in the movies, but it sanded down some of his rougher edges. Before he faded into unconsciousness that final night, he told Rose that she was the only thing he had ever loved that he hadn't over time come to hate.

Living alone for the first time in her life, Rose wasn't sure which puzzled her more, the creature she had seen in the orchard the night Fieldin died or Fieldin himself. She had learned from the letter he left on the bedside table that he wanted to be buried beside his parents, beneath a headstone bearing a Star of David. He'd never even told Rose that he was Jewish. About his history he'd said only that he was born in Vienna, to a long line of devout atheists; that when he was three years old his family had emigrated from there to Cleveland, where his father taught surgery at Case Western; and that his parents kicked him out of the house shortly after he had been kicked out of medical school. Fieldin's mother had still been alive and living in Florida when he and Rose married, but he'd never taken Rose to Palm Beach to meet her (although he went down for a week each February himself) and the old woman had never traveled to the mountains. When Fieldin's will was read Rose discovered that he had left her an investment portfolio—all blue-chip stocks and conservative mutual funds, worth just over $1.2 million—in addition to a small Renoir, which had belonged to his parents and was stored in a climate-controlled vault in Cleveland.

About her Bigfoot sighting, Rose learned that such creatures were routinely spotted in all of the southeastern states—although the orthodox scientific authorities of course denied their existence—and the animals were commonly referred to as skunk apes, because of the broad white or silver vertical stripe on their backs and their notoriously disagreeable odor. Southern skunk apes were generally known to be smaller, but meaner, than their Pacific Northwest counterparts. Rose gathered all this information from the Internet, from a Web site posted by a group calling itself the Cryptozoological Study Association (CSA), which was devoted to documenting the existence of heretofore undiscovered primates south of the Mason-Dixon Line. Studying these reports gave Rose something to think about besides Fieldin, at whom she unexpectedly found herself violently angry. Late at night—when she just wanted to *kill* Fieldin, and was stymied by the fact that he was already dead—she gratefully followed the CSA links to cryptozoological Web sites all over the world. (The Norwegian site had particularly stunning photographs of fjords, although she couldn't understand the text; the Albanian Web site had pictures of naked women smoking cigarettes.) When she gave the CSA a thousand dollars of Fieldin's money, she received an effusive thank-you letter, spattered with exclamation marks, naming her an honorary cryptozoologist.

Most days, she thought that the skunk ape she'd seen in the orchard had been a gentle being, sent by a benevolent god to lead Fieldin to the other side, but some days she couldn't help thinking that its mission had been more malign, perhaps even evil. Either way, it seemed obvious to her that, for whatever reason, that particular skunk ape, on that particular night, had come for Fieldin.

Southern cryptozoologists were divided between the small but harshly vocal faction who thought that in order to convincingly document the existence of an undiscovered species of primate a specimen would have to be killed and the larger but less combative contingent who insisted that the shy, gentle creatures must be protected at all costs. Rose weighed in on the debate by hastily e-mailing a somewhat—she realized later—histrionic letter to the editor of the *Argus,* the local paper, imploring area hunters to let the skunk apes of the North Carolina mountains live in peace. The only noticeable effect that her letter seemed to have on the community, however, was to lead carloads of drunken teenagers to pull into her yard at all hours, beat on their chests, and make monkey noises. She couldn't decide if the kid wearing a gorilla mask who peered in her kitchen window one night was made more frightening, or less, by his fluorescent-orange University of Tennessee sweatshirt. Despite the awful nature of Wayne Lee Cowan's crime—and Rose had never heard anybody, not even the other Cowans, suggest that Wayne Lee *hadn't* blown up that abortion clinic—she found herself feeling a little grateful to him for absorbing, with his continued conspicuous absence, much of the scrutiny and derision that might otherwise have been aimed at her.

Within days of Wayne Lee's disappearance, more than two

hundred state and federal agents had descended on Argyle, followed by a caravan of TV trucks whose drivers thought nothing of taking up three parking spaces at once. The cops rented every motel room in a two-county area and made it virtually impossible to get a table at the Waffle House. An unusually quiet black helicopter circled the mountains day and night, and dangling on the end of a cable extended from its belly was some top-secret doodad of electronic equipment shaped like an upside-down mushroom. Because the sheer number of agents stomping or slinking through the woods made deer hunting a pointless exercise and growing marijuana even more hazardous than usual, and because a large percentage of the agents seemed to possess neither a baseline level of politeness nor a modicum of respect for personal property rights, the FBI soon lost favor with a significant portion of the local population—most of whose Scotch-Irish ancestors had moved to the mountains to escape some type of authority in the first place. Following the detention—by a SWAT team whose members wore ninja masks—of seven-year-old Brian Lee McInerny for aiming a laser pointer at the helicopter, stickers bearing the legend "Run, Wayne Lee, Run!" appeared on telephone poles and stop signs all over town. Not even the million-dollar reward the government offered for information leading to Cowan's arrest noticeably softened public sentiment.

But as time passed, and Wayne Lee Cowan remained at large, the television people and the majority of the cops left Argyle for what they probably considered civilization. Eventually even the remaining skeleton crew of FBI agents decamped as well. Interest in Wayne Lee didn't ratchet up again until the fifth anniversary of the bombing approached. Rose hadn't spoken to anyone in the FBI for over four years when she was visited by D'Abruzzio, the new Special Agent in Charge.

His first name was Richard, but shortly after his arrival he had made the mistake of telling one of the old guys in front of the barbershop to call him Dick. Now he went by D'Abruzzio only, or, when he was pissed off, Special Agent in Charge D'Abruzzio. Rose had noticed him in the Waffle House and found herself sneaking looks at him. He had the knobby biceps of a man who lifted weights for his health and not for his appearance, and he unself-consciously sported the type of virile, dark, vaguely ethnic mustache that most Southern men either wouldn't or couldn't grow.

Late one fall afternoon, D'Abruzzio materialized on her front porch, tapping gently at the screen door; he must have parked somewhere away from her house, an act she found both smart and considerate. They sat at the edge of the orchard, drinking hot spiced cider, while the air cooled around them and the hollows blackened as the shadows pushed the sunlight farther and farther up the side of the mountain. Rose told D'Abruzzio what she and Fieldin had told the other agent: that although Wayne Lee had worked for them, she couldn't honestly say that she knew him, or anything about him.

D'Abruzzio nodded and looked away. He seemed to be thinking about something else. "I read your letter," he said.

Rose felt her cheeks go hot. "Oh, my," she said. "Why on earth are you reading such old newspapers?"

"I like to know where I am," D'Abruzzio said.

Good answer, Rose thought. "Do you think I'm crazy?" she asked.

D'Abruzzio pursed his lips and stared toward the mountain. "No," he said finally. "I don't think so."

"Do you believe in Bigfoot?"

"No comment," he said.

"What's that thing that looks like a mushroom that hangs underneath the black helicopter?"

D'Abruzzio smiled at her. "What black helicopter?"

She blushed again. "You know what black helicopter. The one you brought back with you that doesn't make any noise."

"Ah," he said. "*That* black helicopter. Well, that thing hanging underneath it that looks like a mushroom? I can't tell you what that is."

"I see," Rose said. "A secret. But, hypothetically speaking, could such a thing be used to find a skunk ape? Or, if such a thing was looking for something else and accidentally found a skunk ape, would you be able to tell anybody?"

"I'll make a deal with you," D'Abruzzio said. "I'll tell you if I see a skunk ape, if you tell me if you see Wayne Lee Cowan."

Rose wondered where D'Abruzzio had parked his car, and if anyone had seen it. "Okay," she said finally. "You've got a deal."

D'Abruzzio stood up and stretched. "App Mountain," he said. "Do you know where the name comes from?"

"I always assumed it was short for 'Appalachian.'"

"I wonder," D'Abruzzio said. "Maybe the guy who named it just didn't know how to spell 'Ape.'"

Rose stopped at the foot of Plutina's driveway and stared sadly at her neighbor's house. It was tucked far back up the hollow on a knob its builder must have deemed too rocky to plant. A single light burned in the living room, and a thin gauze of wood smoke hung immobile above the kitchen chimney in the still, dusky air. Charlie had died two months earlier, and Rose knew from personal experience that Plutina was just now crossing over into what would be the darkest days of her widowhood. The officious stream of Sunday-school classes and bereavement committees bearing casseroles and Jell-O molds would begin to dry up, if it hadn't already, and the other visitors would return to their normal pattern of stopping by only when it suited them, if they came at all. Rose collected Plutina's mail from the box and started up the long driveway. Without Charlie and Plutina, she thought, the jagged wind that had swept down the mountain that first winter would have blown her God knows where.

Plutina opened the front door and blinked up at Rose through the screen. Her eyes, magnified as always by her glasses, looked even bigger, though everything else about her seemed to have grown smaller in the last two months.

"Well, Rose," she said. "You might as well come on in."

In the living room she perched in the middle of the couch, her feet barely brushing the floor, while Rose settled uncomfortably into Charlie's recliner. Its cloth upholstery reeked so strongly of cigars that it might as well have been haunted. Above Plutina, Fieldin's mournful Cherokee marched toward one of the mysterious pyramids he had dropped over and over again, without explanation, into Oklahoma.

"Did that FBI man go back to town?" Plutina asked.

Rose grinned. "How did you know he was over at my place?"

"He ain't as smart as he thinks he is, that's how. None of 'em are."

"He wanted to know what I knew about Wayne Lee."

"What'd you tell him?"

"I told him I didn't know anything."

"Good," Plutina said sharply. "That's the right answer."

"I didn't *ask* him to come to my house," Rose said.

"I know you didn't ask him, but he ain't doing you any favors by coming, either. You ought to tell him that."

"I doubt anybody saw him."

"*I* saw him, and I'm half blind."

"Did he talk to you?"

"Not today."

"Do you think Wayne Lee's still alive?" Rose asked.

"I honestly don't know," Plutina said. "I'm just sad it'll be turning off cold again before long. I always hate to think about that boy living out on that mountain in the wintertime." Her shoulders started to shake. She reached into the pocket of her sweater and pulled out a well-used tissue, which she dabbed at the corners of her eyes. "I just hope Charlie's warm."

"Oh, honey," Rose said. "Don't cry."

"His feet are bad to get cold. I used to heat him up a pan of water before we went to bed."

"I'm sure Charlie's feet are fine."

"I don't know what's wrong with me," Plutina said.

"You just miss Charlie, that's all. It'll get better."

"I don't want it to get better. I want it to get over. I've been living up in this valley a long time."

Rose opened her mouth and waited, but no wise words of consolation spilled out.

"I wasn't but sixteen years old when Charlie brought me up in here," Plutina said. "Took me away from my people, but that's the way it's always been when a girl gets married. You know about that. My people are all dead now anyway. We come from over in Weald. My daddy was a town man. He could read good and always knew what time it was. He worked on the railroad."

"Weald," Rose said.

"Me and Charlie never could have babies. Did you know that?"

Rose shook her head.

"I had one, but it was born dead."

"Plutina, I'm sorry."

"After the doctor left, Charlie took it in an old sheet and buried it up on the mountain somewhere. That's the way people did things back then, but it don't seem right to me when I think about it now. All these years I've thought that baby must be wandering around up there, looking for somebody to take care of it. Charlie never even told me where it was. I couldn't go find it if I needed to." She took off her glasses and fished another tissue out of her pocket.

"Well, I'm sure Charlie didn't mean anything by it," Rose said.

Plutina glared up at Rose, her eyes a concentrated blue, smaller and harder than Rose had ever seen them. "You don't know *what* Charlie meant."

Rose stood reflexively. In the foreground of Fieldin's painting, a young Cherokee woman looked at her beseechingly, as if begging her to do something. Rose pointed at the painting. "You're right," she said. "I never understood what Fieldin meant, either. That pyramid."

Plutina blew her nose loudly, but didn't look over her shoulder. "It's a religious picture," she said. "The people are being led into bondage."

Late that night, Rose stood at her bedroom mirror and absentmindedly brushed her hair. Fieldin had been dead for years, and she had resolved some time ago not to cry about him anymore. Enough was enough, after all; he hadn't been *that* nice. But Plutina's spot-on interpretation of his work had simply broken her heart. Of course his Cherokee paintings had been religious pictures. She had just been too literal-minded and, later, too lost in her own work—her popular, sentimental, representational *watercolors*—to figure it out. And Fieldin had been too gracious or arrogant or both to explain it to her, or to anyone else. She could not imagine how lonely he must have felt, driving home from some small-town crafts fair, the car packed with the same canvases he'd set off with that morning. He'd tried, for years and years, to say something he felt was important, and she, of all people, had never even *heard* the story he was trying to tell, much less understood it. She had never for a minute known who he was. If she had only been able to piece the clues together, perhaps she could have helped him. Fieldin had told her that his only memory of Vienna was of sitting in a sidewalk café and watching a small cyclone of dead leaves swirl down the street. He had thought they were birds.

"Oh, damn it, Fieldin," she said. "Why didn't you just say something?"

Rose looked past her shoulder in the mirror to the reflection of the bed they had shared, and willed Fieldin to appear in it. He didn't show, of course—that, at least, was just like him—and the Fieldin she wound up imagining had that awful oxygen tube stuck in his nose. She closed her eyes and listened, but he had stopped breathing all over again. She dropped her brush onto the dresser and walked quickly through the house to the back door, where she cupped her hands against the cool glass of the window and gazed out at the orchard. The light was warm, golden—the gentle light of the approaching harvest moon—but the old trees, stooped again with a harvest of hard, bitter heirloom apples that nobody wanted, looked exhausted by the weight they carried. She found herself staring intently, for no reason she could think of, at the narrow lane of grass between two trees at the far end of the orchard, where it began to slope upward toward the mountain. As she stared, a bulky dark figure stepped out from behind one of the trees and crossed the lane, turning its head toward the house in the instant it took to step across.

Afraid that the creature would hear her open the back door, Rose ran through the house on tiptoe, stopping briefly at the hat rack in the hallway, where she jerked out of her bag the small digital camera she carried with her in case she saw something she wanted to paint. She gently opened the front door and ran down the steps and around the side of the house. She crossed the backyard, keeping the nearest tree between her and the spot where she'd seen the figure, and when she reached the orchard she ran up the lane as quickly and quietly as possible. The skunk ape had come for Fieldin, she thought, and now Fieldin had sent it back. She would take a picture of it and post it on the Internet. She would be a world-famous cryptozoologist. She would get the entire mountain declared a skunk-ape preserve. She would be the goddamn Jane Goodall of skunk-ape studies.

She stopped on the downhill side of the tree behind which the figure had disappeared, her thrashing heart wildly alive in her chest, the dewy grass cold on her feet. She peered into the maze of apple-laden limbs and through a narrow opening saw in silhouette the figure's black shoulder and great, shaggy head. It stood absolutely still. She could just detect a musky, unpleasant, urine-tinged odor. Maybe, she thought for the first time, she would have to go with it. Maybe when the skunk ape came you just had to go. She would follow it up the mountain. She would find Fieldin and kiss him on the mouth and say, Fieldin, you dead bastard. Your paintings, I get them now. I'm sorry. She would be a ghost, if she had to. She would walk the darkest hollows on the coldest nights, singing Scotch-Irish lullabies to Plutina's lost baby. She and Charlie would plant gardens in the forest for the deer to eat. She would paint pictures of the children who lived in Argyle, and leave them tacked to the trees in their yards. And, occasionally, just for fun, she would scare the hell out of teenage boys wearing UT sweatshirts.

Through the tree, she made out the almost inaudible sound of breathing, shallow and fast like her own. The poor thing was as excited and scared as she was. In the distance she heard the muffled, percussive *whup whup whup whup* of D'Abruzzio's black helicopter. Too late, Special Agent in Charge, you with your beautiful mustache. She was ready now. It was time to go to the other side. She wanted to know everything. She looked down, plotting her next step, and on the ground saw a small pile of apples, stacked neatly in a pyramid, waiting to be borne away.

Have You Seen the Stolen Girl?

JESSE JAMES, WHILE hiding from the law in Nashville in 1875, had lived for a time at the address where Mrs. Virgil Wilson's house now stood. For years, Mrs. Wilson delighted in telling trick-or-treaters about the outlaw, but then one Halloween she noticed that the trick-or-treaters did not seem to know—or care—who Jesse James was. They also wore costumes that she didn't recognize and that had to be explained to her—mass murderers, dead stock-car racers, characters from movies she'd never heard of, teenage singers seemingly remarkable only for their sluttiness—and she realized that she had somehow become the crazy old lady whose tedious stories you had to endure in order to get the disappointing candy that such crazy old ladies invariably offered. For how many years, she asked herself, had she been boring children with her tales of Jesse James, and for how many years had they been laughing at her as they walked away? Every Halloween since then, Mrs. Wilson had sat in her kitchen in the dark, listening to the radio at low volume and pretending she wasn't home.

Still, even though several years had gone by since she'd last opened her door on October 31, Mrs. Wilson found herself wondering whether the stolen girl had ever trick-or-treated at her house. "The stolen girl" was how local television reporters had come to refer to Angela B., age thirteen, who had vanished while walking from her house, at one end of Mrs. Wilson's block, to the school-bus stop, at the other. No matter how hard she tried, Mrs. Wilson could not picture the smiling young face she saw on television (and in store windows and stapled to telephone poles and taped to the back windows of pickup trucks and blown up and plastered on the sides of Metro buses) on her own front porch. Whenever, during station breaks, the announcer posed the question "Have you seen the stolen girl?" Mrs. Wilson blinked at the girl's school picture, then shook her head, because she honestly couldn't say.

She liked to imagine that she had once opened her door and found Angela (she would not have been stolen then, so her name would still have been Angela) standing there, waiting patiently, dressed as—what?—a mouse, perhaps, or a rabbit, something soft and nonthreatening. She imagined that she had given Angela not just one or two miniature chocolate bars, as was her habit, but the whole bag, because Angela was clearly such a nice girl and she listened so attentively while

Mrs. Wilson told her about Jesse James. She even asked questions. Mrs. Wilson tried not to imagine anything after the point where Angela said thank you and turned to walk away. The thought of the stolen girl stepping off her porch and disappearing into the darkness inevitably brought tears to her eyes.

Mrs. Wilson's house was equidistant from the stolen girl's house and the bus stop that the stolen girl hadn't reached, and now seemed marked as the place between Point A and Point B where the unknowable existed and the unthinkable occurred. A black hole, the Bermuda Triangle of East Nashville. Four days after the stolen girl had disappeared, and three days after Mrs. Wilson had told two uniformed police officers what little she could, a Metro detective—a sober black woman whose air of professional detachment made Mrs. Wilson even sadder for the stolen girl than she already was—had sat on Mrs. Wilson's good sofa and asked her if she was sure she hadn't seen anything suspicious. Outside, a TV reporter was broadcasting a live report, which Mrs. Wilson and the detective both glanced at from time to time on Mrs. Wilson's muted television. Later, other police officers searched her garage and car trunk and underneath her house for the stolen girl's body. (One of them wriggled out of the crawl space beneath the porch clutching a beautiful cut-glass doorknob, which he solemnly presented to Mrs. Wilson.) The candlelight prayer vigil and neighborhood march organized by the stolen girl's church stopped in front of her house and sang "Where You Lead Me I Will Follow." Not knowing what else to do, Mrs.

Wilson blinked her porch light on and off in what she hoped was a show of solidarity. For days on end, her view of the street was blocked by the satellite-TV trucks parked at the curb, their tall masts raised, their great dishes pointed heavenward, as if awaiting a word from God.

Although months had now passed since the stolen girl had vanished, Mrs. Wilson combed through her memories every day, hunting for the one small clue that might help to break the case and return the stolen girl to her family. What had she seen that day? Surely she must have seen something. The stolen girl jogging past, her books clutched to her chest, chased by a gang of taunting older boys? A van prowling back and forth, its shadowy driver no doubt a religious zealot of some kind, searching for a girl to steal? But Mrs. Wilson remembered nothing of the sort. Increasingly, what she found swimming to the surface of her mind were memories that she had forced herself to set aside years before. She imagined this process to be not unlike that of a police boat trolling the Cumberland in search of one particular corpse and dragging up another instead.

When Mrs. Wilson was fifteen years old and lived in Jackson, Tennessee, she had loved a boy and become pregnant. Her parents had pulled her out of school, and when she began to show, they sent her away to a home in Kentucky, where she lived with two Mennonite spinsters, as lumpen and sexless as sacks of horse feed, and a dozen other "girls in trouble." They were housed in a converted antebellum mansion on top of a hill outside Lexington, but there was nothing in any way grand about the place. Its parquet floors had been covered with gray institutional linoleum, which, although it was already spotless, the spinsters forced them to scrub every day. The girls understood that the endless scrubbing was a punishment of sorts, part of the deal that their parents had struck with the operators of the home, something to make the girls "think twice" the next time they considered climbing into the backseat of a car with a boy. When Mrs. Wilson's baby came, she was not allowed to hold it. She glimpsed the child, a girl, only briefly, as they carried it away, still bloody, its mouth a tiny black O of perfect accusation.

Mrs. Wilson watched the news in Nashville and tried to recall the morning that the stolen girl had disappeared, but instead she remembered the violently blue eyes above the mask of the nurse who had leaned over her as she cried for them to bring back her baby. "Now, sweetheart," the woman had said, "you know you can't take care of a baby."

A week after the baby was born, Mrs. Wilson returned home. Her family pretended that nothing had changed, but, of course, everything had. During her absence, she had become invisible to the boy she loved. She was too embarrassed to go back to school, and her parents didn't force her. Although she was the daughter of a doctor, and spent those long, empty days working on her tan at the country-club pool, she eventually married a poor boy, Virgil Wilson, who was handsome and kind to her and seemed not to notice that she was damaged goods. When Mrs. Wilson came to know Virgil better, she realized that he had considered her a canny choice, a good deal on his part—used, certainly, high-mileage, even, but overall a much better model than he would have been able to afford new.

They moved together to Nashville, where he worked as an electrician. They bought the house at the address that Jesse James had once called home, and they lived there more or less amicably for the forty-eight years it took Virgil Wilson to smoke himself to death. Their only child, a pleasant but wholly unremarkable boy, now lived in Phoenix, where he spoke Spanish like a Mexican and managed a small office for a large company that installed sprinkler systems in the yards of rich people. Mrs. Wilson's daughter-in-law was a vicious anorexic girl from California; her grandchildren couldn't understand her Tennessee accent over the phone. These were the facts of Mrs. Wilson's life, as she now added them up. If she had only been looking out the front window the morning the stolen girl had last walked by, if she had been able to run from the house and scream for the police and save that girl, how different it all might have seemed!

Mrs. Wilson still followed the case avidly on TV, though the reports were less and less frequent. She already knew, of course, that on the morning of the disappearance the stolen girl had been wearing blue shorts, a white T-shirt, and pink sneakers. One night at five, however, she learned that the stolen girl had also been wearing underwear decorated with a picture of Tigger, from *Winnie-the-Pooh,* and one of only two bras she owned. Her other bra remained neatly folded in her top dresser drawer. She had not packed a bag, nor had she removed from her nightstand the cache of sixty-eight dollars that she had earned babysitting.

The next night at ten, a beautiful young woman with perfectly unnatural red hair delivered a report that she, Mrs. Wilson, had watched the young woman tape over and over earlier in the day, apparently trying to get it just right. "For several months in the late eighteen hundreds," the woman said now, staring seriously out of Mrs. Wilson's television set into Mrs. Wilson's living room, "unbeknownst to his neighbors, the outlaw Jesse James lived with his wife and children in the house you see behind me. Now this quiet street bears an even darker secret: what happened to Angela B.?" At this point, the camera zoomed in on Mrs. Wilson's house, and Mrs. Wilson was alarmed to see herself on her own television, peering like a ghost from behind her living-room curtains. "If the people on this street know what happened to the East Nashville seventh grader," the young woman said, off camera, "they're not talking." Mrs. Wilson was aghast. The report was, of course, just filler for a slow news night, but that little bitch had never even asked her if she knew anything! And the actual house that Jesse James had lived in had burned down years before Mrs. Wilson was even born! She made a note to herself to call the station the next morning and complain.

Mrs. Wilson went to bed angry and woke in the middle of the night to find a door that she had never seen before ajar in the wall opposite her bed. She stuck her feet in her scuffs, put on the housecoat that lay at the foot of the bed, and crossed the room. She pushed the door open with the palm of her hand and almost giggled as it creaked melodramatically. Below her, an old wooden staircase disappeared into a dug-out basement. She didn't find it odd to discover a basement in a house that she had lived in for more than half a century, and for this reason alone she decided that she had to be dreaming.

She stepped tentatively onto the top step. It bent slightly under her weight, and she groped around for a light switch, which she did not find. The stairs, though, didn't seem entirely dark, so she took another step down, then a third and a fourth. Soon the staircase opened up entirely on her left (the stairs didn't have a handrail), and, afraid to look down into the space below, she kept to the right-hand side of the steps, brushing the earthen wall gently with her fingertips as she descended. Studying the wall, she made out spade marks left by the man who had dug the old basement God knows when. The air grew cooler. It smelled moldy, unbreathed, perhaps unfit for breathing, and it began, as Mrs. Wilson traveled slowly downward, to take on a faintly rotten odor. She heard her grandmother's voice saying, "Copperheads, Julie, you can smell 'em. They smell like rotting Irish potatoes." And, for the first time, Mrs. Wilson understood that this basement was not a good place, that she would discover nothing here that would make her happy.

At the bottom of the steps, she found herself in a long, narrow room with a dirt floor. Dim daylight made its way in through a row of three filthy transom windows, set in the walls, just below the exposed floor joists of the house. At the center of the room crouched a massive black furnace, which Mrs. Wilson instantly recognized as the coal furnace from the home in Kentucky where she'd spent the final months of her pregnancy. Painted in white letters on the firebox door was the word "Hyde"—the name of the company that had manufactured the furnace—and she remembered sitting on the floor next to it with a sad, long-faced girl from Alabama, sharing a single contraband cigarette. She remembered that the girl from Alabama had pointed at the name on the furnace and said, "That right there is what we're doing." The girl from Alabama lost her baby not long after, Mrs. Wilson recalled, and she never heard from her again. Mrs. Wilson wondered how in the world the furnace from Kentucky had ended up underneath her house, and how much she would have to pay to have it cut up and hauled out. She cautiously approached the furnace, turned the handle, and tugged open the heavy door. As she leaned over to look inside, a voice from behind the furnace said, "It don't work anymore. It ain't hooked up to nothing."

Mrs. Wilson walked around the furnace, where a man sat on a box in the corner in the thin light below one of the narrow windows. He had black hair and a full black beard. A dark bruise appeared to stain his left cheek. His suit reeked of mildew, but tied carefully around his throat was an old-fashioned string tie. Mrs. Wilson understood, without quite knowing how, that the man had been sitting on that box, below that opaque window, for untold years. At his feet lay a moldering pile of something vaguely organic that Mrs. Wilson was able to recognize as a saddle only by its two rusted stirrups.

After a time of staring at the man, her mouth opened in recognition. The man nodded. But when she pointed at him and said, "You're—" he raised his hand and cut her off.

"Don't say my name," he said.

"I won't."

"You have my doorknob."

Mrs. Wilson pointed above her head. "It's still in the house."

Jesse James nodded, as if this were a satisfactory answer.

"What do you know about me?" she asked.

He, too, pointed upward. "Everything," he said. "I can hear you."

She looked up at the exposed joists and above the joists at the thin flooring. A stray nail poked through the boards in a spiky nest of splinters.

"See?" he said.

"What are you waiting for?" she asked.

Jesse James reared back on his box and laughed, a scratchy, ill-used sound that made her flinch. His teeth were yellow and dry-looking, and Mrs. Wilson imagined his mouth filled with cobwebs. "Why, kingdom come, Mrs. Wilson," he said. "Judgment Day. I'm waiting for 'em to roll back the stone."

Beside the outlaw, Mrs. Wilson saw for the first time, there was a perfectly round hole—the entrance to a tunnel—cut into the wall. She felt not exactly a breeze but a slight stirring of air emanating from the hole, and she inhaled again the fetid copperhead smell she'd noticed as she descended the stairs. It was stronger now. She measured the hole silently with her eyes and decided that it'd be big enough to walk through if she hunched.

Jesse James saw where she was looking and shook his head. "I can't let you go in there," he said.

"But I need to go."

"If you go in there, I can't let you come back out."

"Who's in there?" she asked.

"The stolen girl," he said.

"Which one?" she heard herself ask.

Jesse James cocked his head and looked at her quizzically, as if she should already know the answer to the question. "Why, all of 'em," he said.

Mrs. Wilson awoke to find herself clutching her stomach and howling. She climbed out of bed and stormed through the house, doubled over, screaming into a pain that seemed to have no particular locus but flowed from everywhere at once.

"No!" she yelled in the kitchen.

"No!" she cried in the hallway.

In the living room, she collapsed onto her good sofa and wailed, "No! Don't take her. Bring her back!"

She drew her knees up to her chest and sobbed until the pain eased and it was the sobs themselves that had become painful. When she rolled onto her back and stared upward, trying to catch her breath, she was surprised to find that it was morning, that sunlight, indifferent and beautiful, was filling the room, as if all were right in the world. Mrs. Wilson climbed to her feet and staggered to the front door. She took the key from the nail, unlocked the deadbolt, and pulled the door open. She gasped when she saw two little girls, no more than seven or eight years old, heading along the sidewalk toward the bus stop, their arms linked, their heads close together, giggling and whispering conspiratorially. School had started again. A cold shot of adrenaline fluttered into Mrs. Wilson's heart. Nobody was watching the girls. Where were their parents? Where were the police? How could everyone have forgotten the stolen girl so soon? Only a few months had passed, after all, since the stolen girl had walked this street for the last time.

Fifteen or twenty yards behind the girls, an overweight teenage boy clumped along, his black baggy jeans drooping down over the tops of his shoes, some sort of sports jersey hanging almost to his knees. He was looking at the ground, nodding his head to whatever music was coming through the headphones clamped over his ears.

Mrs. Wilson crossed her porch. She stepped down onto the top step and pointed an accusing finger at the boy. "I'm watching you," she called out. "I know who you are. I know where you live. I'll recognize you."

The boy nodded along, oblivious. But out of the corner of her eye Mrs. Wilson saw one of the girls look back. The girl whispered something to her friend, who also glanced over her shoulder at Mrs. Wilson. Then the second girl said something to the first and together they began to run, their book bags bouncing against their backs in a way that looked painful.

Mrs. Wilson clutched the collar of her housecoat and ran a hand through her hair. "No," she whispered. "Oh, no." She took a few hesitant steps down the sidewalk, waving at the girls, as if waving could pull them back, could make them unafraid. "Come back!" she said. "It's not me! I swear. You don't have to be afraid of me!"

Yard Art

SHE LIVED ALONE NOW, in a big house in Brentwood bought with the royalties of a bad country music song her husband had sung. When her husband moved out he had taken the furniture with him—out of spite—enough to fill the six large units he had rented at a place on Gallatin Road. She found that she liked the house without furniture—she had acres of parquet floor on which, after a few glasses of wine, she gleefully slid in her sock feet—but one of the toilets downstairs ran constantly, which drove her crazy. She could hear it all over the house, even when she covered her head with a pillow in the master suite upstairs.

The plumber she called was a singer, of all things—"Arlen Jones, the High Lonesome Plumber," said his ad in the Yellow Pages—and it was the High Lonesome Plumber who now sat backward astride her noisy toilet, working on something inside the tank while she leaned against the doorjamb and watched.

The plumber's pants had not slid down the way one frankly and perhaps unfairly expected a plumber's pants to, but when he leaned over the tank, his golf shirt hiked up his back, and she caught herself staring at the thin column of curly, gray hair that had migrated north of his belt. She looked at her wineglass and set it down on the counter beside the sink. She had no idea why she had called a plumber who wanted to be a singer, instead of a plumber who just wanted to be a plumber, because—for the moment, anyway—she hated all singers and thought that the world would be a better place if somebody invented some kind of bomb to drop on Nashville that would kill all the singers without hurting anybody else. Well, maybe not all the singers. Maybe just the hat acts. That's what Nashville needed—a hat-act bomb. Her soon-to-be ex-husband, the furniture thief, was a hat act.

The plumber put the lid back on the tank, got down on one knee, and twisted the valve open. They listened. When the tank filled, the water stopped running and did not start up again. Her house once again grew cavernous with quiet. He stood and looked at her.

"It was just a seal," he said.

"A seal?" she said, thinking suddenly of ice, of some man in a fur parka looking through binoculars.

He blinked a couple of times, then grinned. "They're bad this time of year," he said. "Them seals."

She covered her face with her hands. Her cheeks were hot. Too much merlot. She wondered if her lips were purple.

The plumber sat down on the toilet and began putting his tools into a canvas bag. He looked up at her and smiled again.

"I'm so stupid," she said.

His brow dipped once, but he didn't stop smiling. "Don't say that," he said. "No reason you should know anything about seals." He jerked his head at the tank. "That kind, anyway."

She wanted to change the subject and—even though she already knew the answer—asked, "Why do you call yourself 'the High Lonesome Plumber?'"

He said, "Oh, it's because I sing a little bit every once in a while. Bluegrass mostly. Some karaoke. I'm a high tenor. You know, like Bill Monroe."

"Oh," she said.

The plumber zipped the tool bag, but made no move to stand. Here it comes, she thought.

"Cammie Carson," he said. "Aren't you—"

"Mrs. Keith Carson?"

He nodded.

"That's me. That's me for now, anyway. I mean, it'll still be me, I guess, but we're getting divorced."

"I read about that."

She had until recently occasionally appeared in magazine and newspaper gossip columns, as in "Keith and Cammie Call It Quits." Now she wasn't anybody important. She shrugged, slapped her hands on her thighs, picked up her wineglass.

"That song was quite a hit," he said. "How long was it number one?"

"Eleven weeks."

The plumber whistled. "Eleven weeks," he said.

The house seemed so unnaturally quiet whenever they stopped talking that she found herself wishing he hadn't fixed the toilet.

"But it's a *stupid* song," she blurted out. "'I Keep My Hat in My Truck.' I mean, what kind of song is that?"

"I wasn't planning on singing it."

"Good. When Keith wrote that song, we didn't even *have* a truck."

They paused for a moment, listening to the song play inside their heads.

"I don't care where he keeps his damn hat," she said.

"All right then," said the plumber, standing up. "If you don't care where he keeps his hat, I don't care where he keeps his hat. That's just the way it'll be."

She turned, walked into the hallway, and motioned for him to follow. "Right this way," she said. "I keep my bag in the kitchen."

She grew self-conscious crossing the living room with the plumber in tow and fought off the urge to break into a run. The room had a floor big enough to hold a basketball court, with a cathedral ceiling high enough for, well, a cathedral. She had noticed that, even when the living room had been crammed with furniture and ficus trees, people had tended to talk in whispers and look for a way out. Ahead of them, down the long hallway on top of the kitchen island, sat the squatty statue of Millie and Joe. Roughly carved out of limestone, about the size of a gallon milk jug, it was her most prized possession.

"What's that?" he asked. "Did you get it in Mexico or somewhere?"

"That," she said, "is Millie and Joe. They're the reason I don't have any furniture."

"How'd that work?"

"Well, when we split, Keith said we had to sell it, and I told him there was no way in hell. Then one thing led to another, I lost my temper, and he got the furniture. And he didn't even want it, the jerk. He *stored* it."

The plumber leaned over and stared closely at Millie and Joe. "I believe I would've rather had the furniture."

"Have you ever heard of William Edmondson?"

The plumber shook his head.

"He was a sculptor, from Nashville, and he was the first black man to have a solo show at the Museum of Modern Art, back in the late thirties. He did this."

"Well."

"He was a genius," she said.

"Okay."

"What don't you like about it?"

"I didn't say I didn't like it," the plumber said, "but it looks to me like he could have done some more carving on it. This thing just barely seems carved out at all."

"That's the whole point," she said. "I mean, look at those

two. You can tell they've been married forever, that they can't imagine waking up without the other one lying right there, but, like you say, they hardly seem carved out at all." She reached out and touched Millie's face with a finger. "Edmondson could do the grandest things with the smallest gestures. I don't know. I just think that's wonderful."

The plumber walked around the island and looked at the statue from the back, then returned to where he had started. The old couple sat with their hands on their knees, their shoulders touching, and smiled as if they had just eaten a particularly satisfying meal.

"I don't know nothing about art," he said, "but they *seem* happy."

"They are happy. And they make me happy. After that damn song went number one, Keith and I bought a whole bunch of stuff, and spent a whole *lot* of money, but this is the only thing we ever bought that meant anything at all to me. I keep it here because that recessed light up above it is the brightest light in the house."

The plumber placed both hands on the counter and turned and stared at her. She thought he looked as if he were in the middle of realizing something important. She imagined he was beginning to understand the gorgeous incongruity of William Edmondson's primitive modernism.

"What's it worth?" he asked.

"Mr. Jones. Be ashamed. I know your mama raised you better than that."

"Well," said the plumber, "all I can say is, Mama tried."

"She didn't try hard enough, apparently," she said, hoping that she had sounded light, but realizing that she hadn't. She almost told him what it cost, by way of apology, but caught herself in time. Millie and Joe had cost $108,000. Telling him would have made her afraid.

The plumber stared into space for a moment, then swallowed. A blush appeared from beneath his shirt collar and rapidly rose up his face. "You know what?" he said. "I know where one of these things is."

The next morning, in the plumber's truck, she stared at the red bandana tied around her right wrist (it matched the one tied Dale Evans–style around her throat) and just felt like crying. She felt as if she had become, at only age twenty-eight, the kind of silly Brentwood housewife who dressed up for plumbers. She could not believe she had tried on more than one outfit. What was wrong with her? She was, she reminded herself, extremely pretty—she had even been declared "gorgeous" by more than one tabloid—and she was rich. She was married, for the time being at least, to a famous singer who was as pretty as she was.

The plumber made her sad, too. He wore a starched white shirt and jeans with creases pressed down the front. A Windbreaker zipped halfway. Tasseled loafers. Date clothes. His truck, not the work truck he had driven yesterday but what she realized now was his *good* truck, had been freshly vacuumed and smelled like pine trees growing in a field of cigarette butts. God, she thought, we deserve each other.

"I've been thinking about what you said yesterday," he said. "About how that Edmondson man did big things with small gestures. You know, Hank Williams wrote songs like that."

She nodded. Keith, like all country singers, paid public fealty to Hank Williams, but privately found his music simplistic and twangy.

"The only thing I know much about, besides plumbing, is music, and I had to put what you said into music terms to understand it. But it makes sense."

The plumber glanced at her. "I burned you a CD," he said.

Please, God, she thought, not a CD. Once Keith's single took off, he hadn't been able to go to the men's room in Houston's without bringing back somebody's demo. Now they were coming after her.

He pointed at the disc sticking out of the dash. "Push that in," he said.

The song was "I'm So Lonesome I Could Cry." The sound was muddy, and the plumber had tuned his guitar sharp, but he had a high, clear, actually lovely voice. She wondered how many times he had sung the song into his computer before he was satisfied with it. When the track got to the part about the silence of a falling star, he tapped waltz time on the steering wheel and softly sang high harmony along with his own melody.

When the song finished, they sat and listened to the CD hiss. The plumber pushed the eject button. She knew this was the part where she was supposed to say, God, that was in*cred*ible, can you send some copies over, I know some people, they're going to want to hear this, *this* is going to blow their minds. But the sad fact was that she didn't really know anybody, except Keith, and the plumber was thirty years too old. She said, "That's a gorgeous song."

The plumber nodded.

She could tell by the look on his face that she had disappointed him, so she added, "You have a nice voice."

"Well, thank you," he said.

"I really don't know anybody," she said. "And they probably wouldn't talk to me if I did."

"That's not why I played it for you," he said. "I know there's not much demand in the industry for fifty-six-year-old bluegrass singers. My ex-wife reminds me of that every time she gets a chance. I just wanted you to hear it."

"Oh. How long were you married?"

"Twenty-seven years."

"What happened?"

"Karaoke, I guess, is the short answer. Too much singing. Too much drinking. Too many women. Too much fighting about drinking and women. Singing don't seem to be a good thing for marriage."

"Singing isn't the problem."

"You're right about that, I suppose. What about you? If I remember right you and Keith got together in high school?"

"Hardin High in Carthage, Tennessee."

They had become "Keith and Cammie" for the first time when they started dating sophomore year. All of this was pretty much public record. Keith's publicists had seen to that. Tiny town. High school sweethearts. The perfect origin myth.

"And you're a nurse, right?"

"Nurse-practitioner. I was a midwife."

She had supported Keith while he bartended and played open mic nights and hung around on Music Row. Then he got his deal at Sony and the song hit. She thought the phrase sounded ominous, like an automobile accident, but decided that was appropriate. She had quit work because of how often she had had to fly to LA with Keith. What a waste of time that seemed now, all that flying to LA.

"So tell me," the plumber said, "what were you like in high school?"

She didn't like his tone and shook her head. This wasn't going to turn into a date.

"Then what was Keith like?"

"Well, he was a band nerd, he played the trumpet, although now he's got God knows how many people trying to keep that hushed up. It's that whole 'Garth Brooks was a decathlete' thing. Apparently you can't be a band nerd and keep your hat in the truck."

"I guess," the plumber said. "Band nerd. What else?"

"What else," she said. "Okay, after Keith got his driver's license, he would come over to my house real early on Saturday mornings, and my parents would give him my car keys, and he would drive my car to his house and wash it. And I would stay in bed and pretend to be asleep until he brought it back. Every Saturday morning he did that. And he did it all winter long, no matter how cold it was."

"That sounds kinda sweet."

"It was sweet." She touched the bridge of her nose with an index finger and closed her eyes and stood for a moment in the window of her bedroom in Carthage, peeking from behind the curtains as Keith pulled into the driveway.

"A long time ago," she said when she opened her eyes, "a long, *long* time ago, Keith Lee Carson of Carthage, Tennessee, was a very nice boy."

That morning, while settling on the bandanas, the chinos, the denim shirt, the leather jacket, and the hiking boots she now wore, she had begun to worry that the plumber might take her off somewhere and kill her. She had tried to dismiss the thought as paranoid—when Keith left he seemed to have taken all the crazies in Nashville with him—but when she saw the plumber's truck pull through the gate, she scrawled his name on a Post-it note and stuck it to the mirror in the bathroom where he had fixed the toilet. She was fine on the interstate coming north. The plumber seemed normal enough, slightly sleazy in the way most of the divorced men she knew were, but, other than that, okay. Once they exited onto Dickerson Pike, though, she started to worry again. The motels they passed had bars on the office windows and signs advertising hourly rates. She saw a prostitute leaning through the window of a parked car. A man with a bright red face and vivid, stricken eyes staggered across all four lanes of traffic.

She began to picture that pretty Greek reporter from Channel Four doing a live report from in front of the woods where somebody—deer hunters, probably—had found her partially clothed body.

"It wasn't always like this," the plumber said, as if reading her thoughts.

"What?"

"Dickerson Pike. It wasn't always like this. It's always been working-class, don't get me wrong, but you didn't used to see all the whores and crackheads and shit like you do now. I wouldn't have brought you over here, but this is where the statue is."

She tried to smile in a manner she hoped made her look brave and game, a formidable person, but in the distance behind the reporter she could see police tape strung through the trees. "Oh well," she said. "I'm glad I dressed for adventure."

The plumber stopped his truck in front of an abandoned bungalow, the last house on a dead-end street in a sad neighborhood south of Dickerson. The windows of the house were boarded up, and somebody had spray painted obscenities and what she assumed to be gang graffiti, or satanic symbols, on the plywood. Briars and broom sedge and young trees grew waist-deep in the small portion of the yard that hadn't been overrun by a marauding privet hedge. The plumber looked around carefully, studied his mirrors, then gunned the truck up over the curb, through the yard, and around the back of the house, where he stopped it out of sight of the street and cut the engine.

"Okay," he said. "Here we are."

She tried to remain calm, but had to concentrate very hard to keep from seeing what lay inside the police tape. Then the plumber reached over, opened the glove compartment, and pulled out a shiny black handgun. She recoiled as if he had magically produced a rat, or a rattling snake. She yanked and yanked on the door handle, but her door would not open. When he touched her on the arm, she pushed herself as far back into the corner as the door would allow her to go and stared wildly at him.

"Oh Lord," he said. "Oh Lord. I'm sorry." He flipped the pistol in his hand until the butt pointed toward her. "Here. You take it. You can carry it. Oh, darlin', I am so sorry."

She looked down at the proffered pistol, and then up at his face. He appeared ready to burst into tears. Please don't cry, she thought.

"Darlin', I didn't mean to scare you, honest to God. But we just ain't in the best neighborhood right now, that's all. I promise. I got a permit."

Without taking her eyes off the plumber's face, she slowly shook her head. "No," she said. "You keep it. I'm all right. I'm fine now."

"You sure?"

"I'm sure. You can stop calling me darlin'."

The plumber smiled a little. "Okay," he said. "Good. I'm sorry about that. I guess I should've told you, I keep my *gun* in my truck."

She didn't laugh. He reached back toward his armrest and pushed a button. She heard the door behind her unlock. He stayed in the truck while she got out and sat on the bumper with her hands on her knees and concentrated on breathing. He didn't open his door until she stood up.

"Tell me where I am," she said. Now that she had convinced herself she wasn't in danger, the adrenaline still coursing through her body made her feel powerful, strong, like a cop at a crime scene rather than a corpse. She wanted to ask questions, get to the bottom of things.

"This house here used to belong to Miz' Louise Twitty. She was a black woman who used to keep me when I was little. Her mama helped raise my mama, and she helped raise me. I rode the school bus here every afternoon until I got old enough to stay at home by myself."

"What happened to her?"

"She died seven or eight years ago. Fell and broke her hip. Almost starved to death before anybody came to check on her. Died in the hospital."

"That's a sad story."

"It is," he said. "It is a sad story. She was a good woman and deserved better."

"And she had an Edmondson?"

The plumber nodded.

"I'm not going in that house," she said. "You can forget about that."

"It ain't in the house. It's back there." The plumber pointed with his chin toward the far corner of the backyard, which, if possible, was more overgrown than the front. "It ain't going to be easy to find, but that's where it is."

She followed him into a small thicket of briars and honeysuckle. He tried to mash the briars down with his feet to clear a path for her. "I had no idea it had grown up like this," he said. "This has all gone to hell. Miz' Louise would pitch a fit if she could see this."

When they neared the back of the lot he slowed and leaned over and began to look around on the ground, as if searching for the tracks of an animal. He pointed out an irregularly shaped piece of limestone. "We're getting there. Gene was standing in the middle of a circle of rocks."

He told her that Gene had been Miz' Louise's husband. He had died at Pearl Harbor, and she had put a statue of him up after the war.

"And there ought to be some seashells up in here," he said. "She put seashells inside the circle since Gene was killed in the Navy. We used to bring her back a sand bucket full from Gulf Shores every year."

She dragged at the honeysuckle and briars with the toe of her boot until, beneath a layer of old leaves and dead vines and briar stems, she saw the white, scalloped back of a seashell. A cold puff of adrenaline squeezed through her scalp and vanished into the air. When she reached down to pick up the seashell, a piece of briar she had been holding back with her foot snapped forward and latched itself onto the back of her hand. "Ow," she said, and jerked her hand away. "Shit."

"Careful," said the plumber. "You all right?"

"Yes, damn it," she said, sucking at the back of her hand. "There's a seashell."

The plumber held his palm flat in front of him and moved it in a circular motion, as if waxing the hood of a car, or divining the area for spirits. "There was a circle of rocks here about five yards across," he said. "And inside the rocks was a layer of seashells. And in the middle of the seashells was Gene."

"Can you remember when Gene was killed?"

"Lord, darlin', I ain't nearly that old. What I do remember is Miz' Louise wearing me out with a switch one time for setting foot inside the circle. She didn't allow nobody inside the circle.

"She used to keep a whole bunch of us little kids, whites and blacks, while our mamas and daddies worked. Before I started school, I don't guess I could even tell the difference between white and black. Them little black boys were the first friends I ever had. But after we got to high school, I wound up fist fighting just about every one of 'em. But they turned out all right. We speak and everything. Most of their kids, though, is on crack."

"You got any kids?"

"I got a daughter."

"Is she on crack?" She asked the question before she had time to consider its politeness and discard it.

"No," said the plumber. "Her specialty is eating Krispy Kreme doughnuts and having illegitimate children."

He kicked at a clump of honeysuckle, and his shoe thudded dully against something solid and hard. He stomped the briars down as best he could, and reached over and jerked at the honeysuckle with his hands. When the vines came away, a small face appeared suddenly between his legs. She leaned over and gasped and clasped her hands together in front of her chin.

"There he is," the plumber said. "Gene."

"Oh God," she said. "Let me see. Let me see."

The plumber knelt down and pulled away the vines still clinging to the statue. What she saw at first was what she wanted to see, an undiscovered statue by William Edmondson, the Edmondson she had planned to steal and display in her house in Brentwood. It took a moment for her to see the cracked and rotting cast-concrete figure actually standing there. Yard art.

"It's not an Edmondson," she said.

"It's not?" said the plumber. "Sure it is. See, he's a sailor. Look, he's wearing a little sailor hat."

She shook her head.

"And look at the suit. Look at the kerchief. And the yoke on his shirt. He's wearing a sailor suit. Gene was a sailor."

"Listen, Arlen," she said. "It's not an Edmondson. It's made out of concrete. It's a replica of the sailor on the Cracker Jacks box."

The plumber sat still for a moment. "Cracker Jacks," he said.

"Cracker Jacks."

"Miz' Louise always said he was looking up at the sky. She said he was looking at the planes and knew he wasn't coming home. She said she could tell that he was thinking about her. But it's the Cracker Jacks guy."

"That makes me want to cry," she said.

"You know, when I was a little fellow, I thought Miz' Louise was already as old as dirt. But she couldn't have been what, forty, forty-five years old? She was still a young woman, but she never married nobody else. She just come out here and looked at that statue."

The face of the statue had worn almost completely away, and what was left was scarred with lichens. Gene stared up in what seemed to her a rigor of anguish. He had known he wasn't coming home, but she was certain his final thoughts had not been of his wife back in Nashville. He had thought instead of burning oil, or of water pouring into the twisted steel room in which he found himself trapped. She could see it in his face. Her eyes filled with tears and she turned away. Miz' Louise had not commissioned a statue from William Edmondson, an old man who believed God had ordered him to carve figures in stone, later anointed a genius by the likes of Edward Steichen; Miz' Louise had gone instead to a gravel lot scattered over with birdbaths and garden benches and fat cherubs, and selected a replica of the Cracker Jacks sailor from a line of identical figures.

She had considered Miz' Louise's story romantic, even mythic, when it contained an undiscovered Edmondson, but now it seemed small and ordinary and so simply and terribly *sad.* There was no other word for it. Had the little Cracker Jacks dog been included in the price? What had Miz' Louise done with the *dog*? She pressed the heels of her hands into her eyes. She cried for Miz' Louise and her cheap statue, and because Keith Carson's money had made her the worst kind of snob. She cried because a long time ago she had loved a boy who had washed her car even though his hands had ached in the cold, but now that boy was dead, as surely as the girl who had loved him. She knew then that she would sell her house and buy a smaller one. She would go back to work and pull babies screaming into the world. She would donate Millie and Joe to a museum, where they would smile out at visitors from beneath a golden beam of light. She would marry a man who would stay with her until she died, a man who would select a stone for her grave from a line of identical, machine-cut stones. Once it was placed at the head of her grave, her name incised on its slick face, he might even consider it beautiful. His grief, she imagined, though remarkable to him, would be ordinary. Her shoulders began to shake. If that's all there was to hope for, why couldn't she accept it as enough? Why couldn't anybody?

The plumber stood up, his back still to her, and stared down at the statue.

"Well," he said. "Fuck."

Just Married

Hardy in the Evening

HARDY AND EVELYN have been married forty-eight years. Evelyn believes the cars passing her house contain secret agents come to watch her, that the boys who play basketball across the road want to see her naked. Her feet inside her bedroom shoes are slowly turning black.

Hardy dabs at a spot on her thigh with a cotton ball dipped in alcohol.

Evelyn says, "You're not trying to poison me, are you, Hardy?"

Hardy thinks, too much medication. Hardy thinks, you are just about crazy. He squints at the numbers on the side of the syringe.

Evelyn says, "It would be easy for you to poison me if you wanted to harm me. You wouldn't ever harm me, would you, Hardy?"

"No baby," says Hardy. "I would never harm you."

Evelyn says, "I know you love that dog more than you love me."

Hardy says, "Hush, hold still."

Hardy was a hero during the war. The first man he killed had leapt out of a foxhole in North Africa and tried to run away. Hardy led him slightly and dropped him like a rabbit. The last man Hardy killed had been taking a leak, in Czechoslovakia, two days before the war ended. Hardy stepped out from behind a tree. The man smiled and said, "No Kraut."

Hardy shot him through the heart. By then he didn't care anymore.

The dog is a Brittany named Belle. Hardy walks her across the yard toward the cornfield that opens up beside his house.

Evelyn yells from the porch, "Where are you going, Hardy? Hardy, you come back here."

Hardy hears the basketball stop bouncing across the road. If he answers, he will not make it into the field. He keeps walking. Evelyn slams the back door. The ball starts bouncing again. At the edge of the field, Belle looks up at him and whines. She is the best bird dog Hardy has ever had. He carries the shotgun only because Belle doesn't like to work unless he's armed. "Hunt," he says, and the dog bounds into the corn stubble.

One night, after Hardy had come home from the war, he woke up out in the yard. He didn't know where he was. Evelyn stood off to the side in her nightgown, calling his name. He moved his eyes toward her but didn't dare turn his head.

"Hardy," she said, "I brought you a blanket. I thought you might be cold." Her nightgown glowed in the moonlight. Hardy motioned for her to get down. Evelyn knelt in the grass. "Hardy?" she said. "It's me. Evelyn. I'm your wife. We're home. I'm not going to let anything happen to you."

As Hardy steps past the dog, two quail explode into the twilight. He intentionally draws a bead behind the nearest bird and squeezes the trigger. The orange flame from the muzzle licks out against the darkening sky. The shot claps and echoes as the birds arc unharmed across the field toward the woods. Hardy hears their wings whir. For a moment he is intensely happy. The dog breaks point and turns and looks at him. "I missed him, Belle. It's my fault, girl. It's all my fault. You did a good job. Hunt."

Back at the house, Hardy discovers four pills inside the dog's bowl: two Elavil, a Lasix, and an aspirin. He imagines Evelyn emptying her medicine onto the kitchen counter, picking through the pills the way a child might choose crayons from a box. Hardy allows his shoulders to shake exactly twice. When he came home from the war, he couldn't hold down a job or sleep inside a house. Evelyn had loved him back into the shape of himself. That she breaks his heart now seems to him only fair. Hardy drops the pills into the pocket of his hunting coat. He walks toward the door slowly, but in a straight line, and does not stop.

Bridge

Ray and his wife, Charlene, have rented a house that looks down onto a small town piled into a narrow gray valley four hundred and fifty miles from home. All the houses Ray can see are built of the same rust-colored brick. His house is that color, too. The great river for which the valley is named flows north; downstream is up on the map, while home, south, lies upstream, facts of geography Ray finds disconcerting.

Ray was a newspaper reporter until he began to forget how to spell. First, he lost track of the number of *r*'s in "sheriff," then he lost the *f*'s. "Commission" began to look right no matter how he spelled it. Charlene teaches information technology at a small Christian college. That's how they came to this little town by the river. She is serious and pale, unashamed to pray out loud in restaurants. Ray stopped going to church with her about the time the letters in the word "Episcopalian" flew apart as if they had been held together by springs. He could still spell "God," but found that he no longer cared to.

Mornings, after Charlene goes to school, Ray lies on the couch and tries to think up ways to make his day seem constructive. He has never bothered looking for work at any of the small newspapers in the valley. He doesn't even know where his clip file is. Afternoons, he walks down the hill into town, where the square, the buses, the restaurants and barber shops are filled with old men waiting to die. The old men once made steel for bridges. This is what they talk about while they wait. The steel they made. They built the bridge that leaps from the town square out over the river. The bridge is green and intricate, held high above the water by four tall, delicate-looking towers.

Ray can see the bridge from his kitchen window. He sneaks into the kitchen forty, fifty, maybe a hundred times a day to look at it, to make sure it is still there. He does not actually expect the bridge to disappear, but still takes a kind of giddy, secret pleasure in keeping watch. Sometimes when Ray looks at the bridge he can feel himself falling toward the river, a sensation he tries to control. He has been told by a trained professional—Charlene's idea—that he is in danger. Ray, however, does not feel as if he is in danger, although he likes the sound of the word. *Danger!* Recently he has begun to feel very light, unencumbered, almost invisible. He sits among the old men in the square and they never look at him. He startles them when he speaks. What is dangerous, Ray thinks, is paying some stranger one hundred and seventy-five dollars an hour—even though the college picks up the tab—for the stranger to tell him he shouldn't be allowed to drive his car, that he might suddenly decide to drive it into oncoming traffic. What the stranger doesn't realize is how much Ray loves his car, even though it is old. He changes the oil every twenty-five hundred miles; his tires are new, French, religiously rotated, precisely inflated.

One evening, after talking to the stranger, Ray tells Charlene he is feeling better. She smiles and suggests he walk down the hill and return the DVD they watched the night before. It is an Italian movie set on a Greek island where nothing bad ever happens. Ray removes the disc from the machine and promises his wife he will be good. Because he did not intend to lie, he is surprised and a little embarrassed when he drops off the movie and heads immediately for the bridge. He knows he will be in big trouble if Charlene catches him anywhere near it, so he hurries. The streetlamps blink and open. He looks down and away from the headlights of the approaching cars.

Ray begins to smile as he turns the corner at the square and starts toward the river. The thought of seeing the bridge up close makes him happy. What he likes about the idea of falling—he has no intention of *jumping,* he is sure of that—is that shortly after hitting the water he will be *somewhere.* Not just in the river, which wouldn't matter, but someplace else. Ray has no idea where that place might be, or if he would even like it, but the existence of so many possibilities so near his house intrigues him. The bridge is a gate, a wardrobe, a looking glass through which he can travel. Ray also knows that his thinking of the bridge as metaphor would worry just about everyone he could think of to tell, so he keeps it to himself. Most people, Ray thinks, are satisfied with simple ideas: bridge as bridge, road as road.

The bridge seems alive when Ray approaches it—resting, breathing, capable of sudden movement. He thinks of a horse, lathered and steaming after a long run, breathing in rhythmic clouds. The hair stands up on his arms. He can't see the river, only the ancient steel curving out over it. Up close the towers are taller than they look from inside his car. Ray walks through a wall of cold air and can now smell the water. He inches forward and reaches his hand toward the bridge's cool, green flank. The steel vibrates beneath his palm. He says, "Shh," and pats the steel. "Shh." The bridge wants him to walk out on it; he can feel it. That's why the old men made it.

What stops Ray from walking out to have a look at the water far below is the guilty thought that Charlene might be coming any minute in the car to find him. This is a scene he wants to avoid. He can easily picture his old car stopped in the middle of the bridge, holding up traffic, while Charlene shouts for him to get in. Ray hates loud noises; he can't stand shouting, horns blowing, the thumping cars of teenagers, the clacking of printing presses, jets passing over his house, and the only thing worse than loud noises is being responsible for them. Ray pats the bridge again, gently, acknowledging the secret regret they share, and turns to face the line of headlights moving toward the river from the square. Beyond the square, more headlights sniff down the hill on which he lives. One of the cars could be his, with Charlene driving, leaning forward over the wheel, her head filled with God and binary codes and concern. Ray jogs until he reaches a place where he could explain his presence. He considers himself a good husband, a man of responsibilities, a right-thinking man.

When Ray gets home, Charlene is making supper. She seems glad to see him, not alarmed that he has been gone too long. She does not suspect him of sneaking off to the bridge because he promised her he wouldn't. Ray is touched by her simple trust. He considers himself the recipient of a small gift—a seashell, a marble, a stick-man made of pipe cleaners. He smiles and gives her a kiss. He can have a look at the bridge again tomorrow while Charlene is teaching. She will never know. Ray asks what's for supper. He glances briefly at the thin face staring back at him from the kitchen window while he washes his hands. The face irritates him because it keeps him from seeing, down in the valley, the headlights crossing and crossing the dark bridge. He sets the table, draws two glasses of water from the tap, and joins Charlene in the dining room. She bows her head and over their married meal offers an earnest prayer, thanking God for all the blessings of the day.

Meteorite

Harris, his hair gone gray—if you can believe that—gardens for Lula because he still misses his mother, who was Lula's best friend. Harris went to school with Lula's oldest son, Willie, who died of pancreatic cancer seven years ago.

Lula does not ask Harris to garden for her; Harris will not accept pay.

Lula sits on the porch and watches Harris working in the field across the road. He is a tall man wearing overalls and a straw hat. From a distance, he could be her son, her husband, her father-in-law—all tall men, farmers, all dead now—and sometimes she secretly allows herself to imagine that he is one or all of them. Her husband, Will, has been dead now not quite two months. Lula doesn't feel sad anymore so much as empty, like a gourd. That's what she told the girls. She feels like a gourd hanging from a barn rafter, waiting for someone to take it down and make something out of it. Perhaps a house for purple martins.

This evening, Harris is hoeing on the far side of the field, close to the woods where the meteorite hit. Lula closes her eyes and wills herself to forget that Harris is Harris, that he has arthritis in his shoulder, and remembers and remembers until she becomes a young woman again, twenty-two, twenty-three years old, a blooming thing, a peach, most of her life still ahead of her.

She stands between Will and Willie, at the edge of a large round hole. The hole is perhaps a foot deep, seven or eight feet across. Willie holds her hand. He is two, maybe three, her first child, and Lula loves him as she has never loved anything in her life. She loves Willie so much that she wants to make another baby every time she lays eyes on Will. She is as happy as she will ever be.

Her father-in-law, Bill, of whom she is affectionately afraid, squats in the hole, pointing at the meteorite. It is about the size of half a brick, the color of a terra-cotta pot, burned looking.

"It's a falling star, Willie," Bill says. "It fell out of the sky."

Willie tries to hide behind her leg.

Will says, "I wonder why we didn't hear it coming? I wonder why we didn't hear it hit?"

On the porch, Lula opens her eyes. She remembers that the meteorite stayed for years in the tool cupboard in the dining room. When Will sold the cupboard, she put everything in it into the hall closet. He'd used the money from selling the cupboard to have indoor/outdoor carpeting put down in the hallway. It seems a poor trade now.

Lula carries the boxes one at a time from the closet to the dining room and empties them onto the table. Inside the boxes she finds the creosote-and-sweat smell of the cupboard, which she had almost forgotten. She finds old pieces of harness, coffee cans of nuts and bolts and washers, three broken hammers, a tangled ball of baling twine, collars from dogs long since dead, an emery stone, a hand drill still clutching a broken bit—all told the midden of a working farm in another time—but she doesn't find the meteorite. Disappointed more than she would have thought, Lula wonders if she has made the whole thing up. She wonders where she will find the energy to put the junk back into the boxes, and the boxes back into the closet.

Harris appears in the doorway and Lula studies his leathery face, the wrinkles around his eyes. How in the world has he gotten to be so old? He glances at the junk spread out on her white tablecloth, the greasy cardboard boxes lying on the floor, but he is too polite to say anything.

"I was looking for something," she says.

"Well," Harris says. "I found you something." He drops the rivet from an overall bib into her hand.

Lula wets her finger and rubs the tarnished piece of brass. Will was always bad about popping the rivets on his overalls. It had bothered her at the time, how, unlike buttons, she couldn't sew the rivets back on. But now, as she closes her fist around it, she feels her heart streaking through space, young again, shedding years as it lights up the precincts of the past.

Honeymoon

Late one night, the summer Ray and I finally made it back south, to Tennessee, we saw a deer standing on the traffic island at the end of our road, and a car coming up the highway. The deer fidgeted and leapt into the light.

By the time we made it over to the wreck, the old man had turned on the hazard lights and the old woman had called 911. He held on to the wheel with both hands, as if the car were still moving, as if it were still possible to drive it, and stared straight ahead through the webbed glass of the windshield. The deflated airbag lay in his lap. I leaned into the window beside him. Ray went around to the old woman. On her knee was a large drop of blood shaped like an apostrophe. It was hard not to look at it, the apostrophe; I waited for it to run down her leg, but it never did.

"Hey, folks," Ray said, as if he had known them forever and had bumped into them at the mall.

The old woman smiled at Ray, and then at me, and said, "Oh, hello, you two." She apparently shopped at the same mall as Ray.

I smelled the gas from the airbags and was afraid for a moment the car was going to explode. I said, "Are you all right?"

"I've been better," the old man said. "To tell the truth about it."

"Oh, it's only a car," she said. She patted his hand.

"We just got married," he said.

"This evening," she said. "In Asheville."

"Really?" I said. "Well, congratulations."

"We stayed too long at the reception," the old woman said. "Everybody was there. All the grandkids. His and mine. We didn't want to leave."

The old man almost smiled. "Well," he said. "We did and we didn't."

"That's true enough," she said. "But we had a grand time."

"Where y'all headed?" Ray asked. He's always been a big question asker, and some days it strikes me as charming.

"Memphis," the old woman said. "We're going to take a paddle wheel all the way down the Mississippi River to New Orleans. I've always wanted to do that. Tonight, though, we just wanted to make it as far as Monteagle."

"That sounds exciting," I said. "I really like New Orleans."

"It's a good town," Ray said. "But it gets hot."

"We've been married for a hundred years," the old man said.

"Just not to each other."

"I was married forty-nine years. She was married fifty-one."

"That makes a hundred. Isn't that something?"

Ray whistled.

"That's something," I said.

"We were high school sweethearts," the old man said.

"We just didn't get married."

"Not until tonight, anyway."

"Because of the war."

"I was in Europe. France, mostly. North Africa, Italy, Germany, Czechoslovakia, all over."

"That's why we didn't get married. He went overseas."

"I got drafted and had to leave before we figured things out."

"We didn't get anything decided," she said.

"And when I came back, she was married. Will didn't have to go because he was deaf in one ear."

"Oh, Hardy, you make me sound so awful. It wasn't like that. You and I just never decided anything."

"I didn't mean it like that. I knew Will. We played softball against each other in the church league, and I used to run into him every once in a while at the feed store. He was a good man, kept a good farm."

"And Evelyn was a good woman. I always liked her, although I never knew her very well. But we always spoke when we passed."

"I was always faithful to Evelyn."

"Of course you were, Hardy. Everybody knows that."

"We were married forty-nine years and I was always faithful."

I looked at Ray and raised my eyebrows. I felt as if they had forgotten we were there, that even if we had walked away they would have been happy telling their story to each other.

"Evelyn and Will died last year," the old woman said.

"Within a week of each other."

"Isn't that odd?"

"Then one day I just up and wrote to her. And she wrote me back and said she had been thinking about writing to me."

"And I was. Isn't it funny the way things work out? Sometimes you can almost see the plan."

"I still have her letter. It's in my suitcase. In the trunk."

"I put his letter in my safety-deposit box."

"Oh, Lula, it's just a letter."

"Not to me."

I almost teared up, imagining the letters—his on plain, white typing paper, hers on cream-colored stationery that smelled like potpourri.

"Nobody writes letters anymore," Ray said.

"Isn't that the truth?" the old woman said. "Years from now, what's going to be left for people to read?"

The old man tapped the steering wheel once with his forefingers and looked first at Ray, then at me. He took his wife's hand. "Let me tell you two something," he said. "I always knew this girl right here was the one. I was married forty-nine years, and I loved Evelyn, but I always knew Lula was the one."

"And I felt the same way about Hardy. I always knew that he was the man for me."

I glanced up at Ray and wondered if he was the right man, or if there was a better man, a better life, waiting for me out there beside some other road. And I could tell that Ray was wondering the same thing about me. Early in our marriage he had almost jumped off a bridge into the Ohio River. And those days had been so hard that sometimes I wished I had let him. But where would I have been the night the old man and the old woman ran over the deer on their honeymoon?

The old man laughed. "Honey, we should probably be more careful," he said. "These two might be secret agents."

"Charlene and I *are* secret agents," Ray said, "but we're on the same side as you." He held up his left hand. "We've got the secret decoder rings."

The old woman winked at us in turn. "We're only telling you our secrets because we don't know you."

"Thank you," I said. "For telling us."

She suddenly slapped her thighs. "But you know what? I think it's lovely that I got to love two men in one lifetime without doing anything bad. I'm not ashamed of saying it. I'm sorry, but that's just how I feel."

"I'm just glad one of them was me," the old man said.

When the ambulance came, Ray and I walked up the highway and looked at the deer. It had slid on its side, turning slowly, almost beautifully, maybe fifty yards up the road. A sharp piece of bone stuck out of one of its legs. The dull eye staring up at us did not seem to have ever belonged to anything alive. We stared back at the deer, and we sneaked looks at each other. We didn't talk. We could hear small living things moving beneath the leaves in the woods behind us. We could hear the katydids and the crickets and the tree frogs and the night birds calling out, all the breathing creatures looking for something in the dark.

Jack and the Mad Dog

JACK, *THAT* JACK, the giant-killer of the stories, spent the better part of the evening squatting in the blackberry briars opposite the house of a farmer's wife who would—for four dollars, but with no particular enthusiasm—lean over her husband's plow and let a boy have a go. She was to step into her yard and fling a rock across the road when her husband went to sleep; Jack was to meet her behind the barn, money in hand. This farmer's wife was widely known to possess both a strong arm and noteworthy accuracy, and, to the rabble who frequented the briar patch, her flung invitations often seemed more punitive than hospitable. So Jack waited in the briars, the black shapes of the berries plain against the less black sky, the berries not quite ripe, on a spot in the dirt worn bare by waiting farm boys, the summer air as close and fetid as the breath of a cat. He tried not to think about the whore-flung, judgment-seeking meteorite that might at any moment drop out of the sky and render him senseless. He waited and drank odd-tasting white liquor out of an indifferently washed Mason jar until he came into a cloudy, metallic, buzzy-headed drunk.

The liquor had been a welcome, if, as it turned out, not entirely pleasant surprise. He had found it sitting upright in the middle of the road, the lid of the jar screwed on tight, as he had set out on his carnal errand. Jack had often found along the road the things he needed most in his travels, so he assumed he needed the moonshine as well. It had smelled all right enough, just a little off, overcooked maybe, and he took a drink. When he did not die or get carted off by witches he took another. Now he squatted and waited and drank, sucked on the sour berries, flinching beneath his hat every time he thought about the rock with his name on it, until both feet went to sleep and the mosquitoes found him in his unlikely lair, thinking: I'm Jack, *that* Jack, the giant-killer of the stories, and my life has come down to *this.*

And still the farmer's wife did not sling her stone: her husband, the farmer, did not grow sleepy. Jack watched the man smoking on the front porch; the red eye of his homemade cigarette stared out toward the blackberry briars from which Jack stared back with increasing agitation. The farmer's shape was distinct, the outline of his work hat sad and plain, lit by that single, small flare, which—the more Jack drank—began to leave fire trails in the darkness as the farmer moved the cigarette between his mouth and the spot where he rested his hand on the arm of his chair. The farmer smoked, one cigarette after another, until the hour grew late and the night grew long, until the katydids tired of their chanting and the crickets tuned down, until all hope passed away from the world, until Jack's hooch and patience dripped away, until that, finally, was that. Jack drained the last of the liquor out of the jar, grimaced, retched, swallowed bile, bad liquor, and a gutful of green blackberries. He stood up, the briars ripping at his clothes, and with a great shout of what he meant to be a curse (but came out instead as an animal blare that made no sense at all, not even to him) he threw the empty jar across the road toward the farmhouse, where it landed in the yard without even breaking.

Jack cocked an ear, listened, waited for the man on the porch to curse back, to yell "Who's out there?" to fire his shotgun into the darkness, to storm down off the porch spoiling to fight the man who had come sneaking onto his property to buy a four-dollar piece of his wife. But the farmer did not make a sound, did not move, sat instead smoking on his porch, placid as a steer, shallow as a mud hole, as if strangers shouting from the briars and Mason jars falling from the sky were every-night occurrences. Jack thought about killing the man—for in the stories he had occasionally killed regular men, but those men had been robbers and millers and the like and had therefore needed killing. He had never killed a farmer, and the one parked on the porch offered Jack no real excuse to start now. He didn't stand up, didn't speak, didn't flick his cigarette into the yard, nothing.

Son of a bitch, Jack thought, he's sitting over there chewing his cud. It was more than Jack could bear. "Cud chewer!" he yelled.

"Go on home, Jack," the farmer said from the porch.

"How do you know it's me?" Jack called. At the time he considered this a clever question.

No response came from the porch.

"How about I come over there with a silver ax and chop your head off?"

"You ain't gonna do no such a thing, Jack. Go on home and get in the bed."

"How about I send my magic beating stick over there to beat you about the ears until you run off down the road and nobody never hears from you again? Then you'll be sorry!"

"Jack," the farmer said patiently, "everybody knows you ain't got no magic beating stick no more. You ain't had one since I don't know when. Now, head on out."

"I'll..." Jack said, considering as he spoke an unexpectedly depleted list of options. "I'll come over there and play a trick on you! I'm still smarter than you are!"

"Not tonight, you ain't. I'm on to you and your sneaking *that* Jack ways. There ain't gonna be no Jack tale around here tonight."

"Ha!" Jack hollered. "There already is! And you're in it! It just ain't a very good one!"

"I'll grant you that," said the farmer.

Jack stood quietly for a moment. "Oh come on," he pleaded. "Just one little slice. All you have to do is go to sleep.

It's late. Ain't you got milking and plowing to do in the morning? Ain't that rooster gonna flap up on the fence post and crow before you know it?"

"Jack..." the farmer chided sadly.

"What?"

"Don't beg. You used to be somebody."

Disappointed in more ways than he could count, drunk but not pleasantly so, both legs asleep all the way up to his hipbones, Jack climbed from the briars and set out. He was not, so far as he knew, setting out to find a job of work, or a maiden to seduce, or new ground to clear. He was not even leading a cow. He did not expect that he would, at the end of this setting out—sordid though it was—encounter an imbecilic king, inexplicably enraged at the sight of Jack whistling down the road; or a giant greedily clutching a gold-shitting goose in an improbably suspended castle; or a coven of witches yowling from a derelict mill in a fury of feline estrus. He did not, to be honest, even feel like fooling with kings and giants, each of whose slayings—despite the inevitable mental and physical challenges such killings called for—still amounted to nothing more than a job of work, but thought it might be okay to taunt and kill some witches once he sobered up, especially if they were good-looking, although he could not remember the last time he had seen a witch, good-looking or not. The witches had gone off somewhere, along with the silver axes and his magic beating stick and the geese and the giants and the swaying beantrees; along with the kings and their bejeweled, creamy daughters and glittering hoards of gold. Tonight all he had was the setting out itself. So he set out.

He trudged along, intent on forgetting his lust for the doughy expanse of the farm wife's lunar bottom, his squatting in the briars like a stray dog waiting to steal a scrap, his rising black hatred of farmers and all things agricultural, until he stepped unexpectedly into a compensatory truth: he could see in the dark. In a single miraculous moment the road beneath his feet, virtually invisible the moment before, unspooled into the distance before him, silvery and faintly glowing, a still river lit by stars or the thinnest sliver of moon. Yet the sky contained neither stars nor moon, just the low black night pushing down.

"Huh," Jack said.

He could see the tall corn on both sides of the road attentively pressing in; he could see not only the wooded ridges which bordered the fields, but also the thick summer foliage, billowed and full, blooming on the ridges' steep sides; he could see the ancient, giant-trod mountains in the distance beyond the ridges, separated from the black of the sky by faint bands of light which shimmered and held colors Jack could not name, colors that vanished if he looked at them directly—angels or ghosts or shy, pale brides undressing in darkened rooms. The light wasn't dawn, or even the idea preceding dawn, which still lay hours away, but something Jack had never seen before, something he was sure no one else had ever seen, either, something that only he could see: the world itself was lit from within. The ridges glimmered, the corn in the fields, the road, the mountains, everything he could see gave off a secret light. When he held his hand in front of his face, it, too, shimmered, and he studied it, his good right hand, a fine thing, well-shaped and strong, a hand as adept at caressing a virgin as plunging a silver sword into the disbelieving eye of a giant. All around his raised hand, wherever he looked, the world revealed itself the way Creation must have revealed itself to God, everything part of the greater light, and it was good, and he stood there dazzled and proud and happy, once again Jack the giant-killer, the best man in the world.

So he whistled along, twirling his Saturday hat on his finger, hoping now for a taller tale, until he reached a good-sized creek spanned by a narrow bridge. As he stepped onto the planking he savored for a moment a breath of vestigial excitement, the anticipation he had once felt every time he crossed a bridge. Perhaps this first step would presage not only a pedestrian traveling from here to there, but a crossing over from this into that, a passing into proper story. He hoped briefly for a troll to flummox, but remembered that trolls were now extinct, save for a non-breeding pair locked up in a zoo in Romania.

Jack was halfway across the creek when a large black dog rose up out of the bridge, simply squeezed itself into being out of the bridge's black wood. Jack pulled up fast. He wasn't afraid—startled a little, maybe, at the dog's sudden appearance, but not afraid. Over the years he had learned that nothing really bad ever happened to him, that he was impervious to injury, if not embarrassment, no matter how formidable the adversary or unexpected its appearance. Learning that he didn't have to be afraid had, however, in an almost tragic irony, also robbed him of the corollary excitement. Why, the last time he had rousted out a giant—however long ago that had been—it was all he could do to make himself run.

"Grr," said the dog.

"Howdy," said Jack. (It was his experience that sometimes animals could talk, and sometimes they couldn't, but that it always paid to find out.) He could see the dog's white teeth as it snarled, could see its slobber-lapping, lengthy red tongue.

"Hello, Jack." The dog had a low voice and spoke wetly, deep in its throat.

"So tell me," Jack said, noting that the dog knew his name, but still wanting to get on with things, "why are you impeding my progress across this here bridge?"

"Because that is my solitary calling."

"Where'd you come from?"

"I'm not sure. It was elsewhere or about, but that is all I can know."

Jack nodded. "Limited omniscient narrator," he said. "My point of view."

"Don't rub it in."

The two spent an expectant moment in silence, as if they were actors strutting and fretting, each thinking that the other had forgotten the next line. Jack finally clamped his hat on top of his head.

"Well, Skippy, or whatever your name is," he said, "this has been interesting and all, but why don't you step to one side and let me pass so I can get along with my setting out?"

"I'm afraid I can't do that."

A flicker of impatience flared distantly behind Jack's eyeballs. He remembered that he was still drunk, but not pleasantly so; that the farmer, simpleton though he was, had smoked him out of dipping his wick; that the summer night was still chokingly close and humid. A liquorous headache began to mold itself into something that felt like a thumb, and to jab repeatedly against the backside of his forehead bone.

"Look," he said, pinching the bridge of his nose, "I don't know what kind of story you think this is, but I can see in the dark, and I was enjoying it, even though I'm drunk but not pleasantly so, and I don't want to fool with no talking dog."

"You don't have any choice," the dog said.

"What do you mean, I ain't got a choice? By God, I'm *Jack*. I've always got a choice."

"Not tonight you don't. I'm going to bite you before you get off this bridge. That's how this story goes."

"Shit," said Jack. "You ain't going to bite me."

The dog sank into a crouch. "Jack, I was put on this earth to bite you."

"Whoa, now," Jack said, spitting out a laugh as if it tasted bad. "You ain't supposed to *bite* me. There ain't never been nobody to *bite* me, not ever, in lo all these many years."

"Grr," the dog said.

"Wait a minute," Jack said. "Just hold what you got and let me think." His setting out had arrived at an arrival he was unprepared to ponder. He hadn't met an old man on the road to tell him he would meet a dog on a bridge and give him a silver sword or magic words with which to kill it. (Jack had always counted on the utilitarian, if narratively implausible, appearance of the old man bearing implements and instruction, but somewhere along the way the old man had disappeared, too.) He was by himself in the middle of a bridge in the middle of the night, beset with tiredness and discouragement. His mind was lightly fogged by odd-tasting liquor, and he struggled to think of a way to outsmart a talking dog. He looked around. There wasn't even a non-magical stick lying about, or a tree to climb in the corn bottoms. Still, in his younger days this problem wouldn't have given him pause. Come on, Jack, he thought, you're *Jack*. Think of something.

"This is the last Jack tale," the dog said, inching closer. "The end of the story."

Jack backed up a step. "Just hold on there, Spot. Before you bite me, I need to know something. Are you mad?"

The dog stopped. "Angry? Somewhat, I suppose."

"No," Jack said. "I mean rabid."

"Hmm," said the dog. "I think so, yeah. I feel a little hindered in the hindquarters."

"So once you bite me I'll die a slow and excruciatingly painful death."

"That seems to be the idea."

Jack frantically searched through his overalls but found only four dollars. He didn't even have a pocketknife.

Without further warning the dog scrabbled forward and

leapt at Jack, who managed to take a step backward as it leapt and wrap his hands around its neck mid-leap and keep it at arm's length; he fell down on top of it, pinning the dog's head and chest to the bridge.

"Ow," said the dog.

As the dog jockeyed with its back legs, trying to find purchase, Jack squeezed its neck as hard as he could. Each of his fingers sought its correspondent on the other hand and interlocked as if playing the child's game of building a church. (Here's the people, Jack thought.) He felt the dog gathering its front legs underneath its body, testing Jack's weight. Jack soon realized he could neither choke the dog to death nor hold it for very long. It was one big dog.

"Damn you, dog," Jack panted. "You should *not* have done that." He felt the dog calmly push up against his chest, preparatory to bucking him off.

"You're done," the dog said. "Once I stand up, it's all over."

"I am not *done,*" Jack said. "For the last time, I am JACK!"

"Which means nothing."

"I'm important to people."

"Not anymore. Not in any substantive way. The day is soon coming when your stories will be told only by faux mountaineers in new overalls to ill-informed tourists at storytelling festivals."

"Well, what's wrong with that?"

"It's *ersatz,* Jack."

"I don't even know what that means."

"It means you're dead already and you don't even know it."

When the dog pushed itself to its feet, Jack grabbed a fistful of fur in each hand. He spun in a tight circle, lifted the dog off the ground by its head, and with a great shout he threw it off the bridge.

Then Jack ran.

By the time he heard the dog crash into the tangled hell of laurel on the creek bank he had already left the bridge behind. Jack didn't know where he was going, only that going seemed to be a good idea, that his setting out needed to be speeded up. Hiding seemed advisable. He ran a few steps down the road, angling toward the creek bottom, gaining speed with each stride, and leapt from the road, over the gully, his legs running through the air, his arms waving in a vain search for flight; he landed on both feet in the sandy soil of the bottom, and with another step crashed into the thick corn. Behind him, he knew, the dog would soon struggle up through the matted underbrush along the creek bank and set itself on his trail.

The corn was fully tasseled, six and eight feet tall, its ears hardening, two hot weeks away from coming ripe. It reached out and grabbed Jack as he fought through it; it struck at him with its thin, pointed fists; it slid its thick stalks and ropy roots beneath his feet to trip him; it became a congregation of angry Baptists—preachers and deacons and teetotalers and desiccated spinsters and dentists and disaffected, undipped Methodists, rattling with judgment and contempt as he fought through it.

Jack, the corn called in multitudinous chorus, *you're a fornicator and a murderer and a thief!*

"Let me go, corn!" Jack spat. He lowered his head and struck back wildly with his arms.

And you're a ne'er-do-well and a swindler and a liar!

"I am *not* a swindler!"

The truth is not in you, Jack! For shame! Why, you swindled your own brothers!

"They had it coming."

You disappointed your mother.

"Don't you talk about Mama."

Repent! cried the corn. *Repent!*

"Go shuck yourself," snarled Jack.

Behind him he could hear—or thought he could hear, imagined he could hear—the dog huffing with deadly inevitability, bulling after him in a rabid, straight line.

Jack fled and fought and cursed with the rage of the unredeemed and the panic of the pursued. He struggled through miles and hours and years and lifetimes of corn and space break and the exposition implied therein, and imagined with each step the rabid fangs of the black dog inches from his hamstrings. After an age and a day he crashed suddenly and unexpectedly out of the corn and sprawled headlong into a prairie of golden wheat. For a long moment he lay facedown on the ground, his nose filled with the rich, anesthetic smells of earth and grain, and considered falling simply into sleep, dog or no dog. He had come a long way. But as soon as he thought about the death that awaited him should the dog catch him—or any death at all, for that matter—he climbed wearily to his feet and stared toward the horizon, where he could at least make out a tree line, no more than a smudge between the field and the sky, who knew how many miles distant, but a destination to aim for nonetheless, a place to flee to. He took a first leaden step toward the trees, and a young girl, maiden age, sprang with a yelp from the wheat in front of him and lit out across the field. Before Jack could even cry out, the wheat around him exploded with girls—hundreds, thousands, multitudes of girls—flushed like succulent quail, bounding toward the distant trees. They cried out, "Help me! Somebody help me!" as they leapt gracefully through the wheat.

Maidens! Jack thought, breaking unconsciously into a jog. Look at all the maidens!

Maidens with glowing complexions of peach and cream and alabaster and ivory, clad uniformly in simple country dresses of virginal white, each dress cut perhaps a size too small and a smidge too short; maidens whose firm flanks fetchingly swayed and flounced, their downy bosoms heaving and swelling; maidens whose flaxen and wheat and chestnut and mahogany and ebony and sable and scarlet and crimson hair billowed and flowed and streamed out behind them; maidens whose panted exhalations were sweet and soft and breathy and catching; maidens whose mysterious and dark and depthless and cerulean and emerald eyes were flashing and shining. In other words, lots and lots of maidens. Tired no longer, Jack vaulted youthfully into full pursuit. He loved nothing more than maidens. He crazily wondered if it were possible to herd all of the girls into one place, like a pasture, or a feedlot. "Hey!" he called. "Come back!"

Jack soon gained ground and fell in behind a pair of twins whose fair hair cascaded behind them in fragrant waves. The girls capered and frisked in step; their silken hair undulated in hypnotic unison. Jack watched their hair for some distance—the girls seemed to have no idea that he was there—but the moment his eyes strayed below their narrow waists the girls stopped and whirled on him so quickly that he almost crashed into them. He managed to bring himself to a teetering, arm-waving halt.

"What do you think you're doing?" asked one.

"Doing?" Jack panted. "I'm running away from a black dog that can talk. What do you think I'm doing?"

"That's not what she meant," said the other. "What she meant was, 'What do you think you're looking at?'"

"Looking at?" Jack said, averting his eyes. "I'm not looking at anything."

"Liar," said the first.

"You were looking at our fair nether parts," said the second.

"Asses," said her sister.

"I was not."

"You were, too."

"Then tell me *this,*" Jack said shrewdly. "If you were running *away* from me, how can you *know* I was looking at your fair nether asses?"

"Because we know, Jack. We *know.*"

"You think we don't know, but we know."

"Girls always know."

"Hmm," Jack said. "I guess I knew that."

"Next you're going to look at our breasts," the first said.

"I am not."

"You are, too," said the second.

The twins stared at Jack until he blinked. Then he looked at their chests. He tried not to, but he did. And there they were, maiden bosoms. Downy. Tumescent. Firm. The ripe pomegranates of the Old Testament. The top buttons of the girls' dresses strained nobly to restrain them.

Jack thought, *Dah-um*. He thought, *God Almighty,* italics his. He felt his manhood stirring. Or his loins. He could never tell them apart.

"See?" said one.

"Told you," said the other.

Jack smiled what he hoped was an old-fashioned Jack smile. "Do I know you?" he asked.

"Do you know us," said one, shaking her head sadly. "Do you know us."

"Oh, you know us," said the other. "The first time we set eyes on you, you came whistling down the road, looking for a job of work, after your setting out."

"You had the dinner your poor, old mama made for you slung over your shoulder on a pole. But the dust on the road had made you powerful thirsty and you had not a drop to drink."

"Mama never remembered to send along water," Jack said. "It was a shortcoming."

"You came upon me first. I was sitting by the roadside, weaving a basket of golden straw for to carry eggs to the market. You asked me to draw you a dipper of water from the well."

"And *I* was sitting in the doorway of our daddy's sturdy cabin, churning a bait of butter for to bake a cake. Then you asked *me* to draw you a cup of water from the well."

"You sure did drink a lot of water."

"Was your daddy a farmer?" Jack asked.

"Miller," said both.

"Ah," Jack said. For one sweet moment he sensed more than remembered the rhythmic rumble of a turning wheel, the gentle *shush shush shush* of water splashing, a slant of silver moonlight, an intake of breath as soft as the noise made by the wings of a moth, but he couldn't conjure the face of a girl. So many maidens, so many mills. Twins, though. He thought he would've remembered twins.

"That night at supper, while our daddy was eating his vittles and eyeballing his shooting-gun leaning by the doorstop, you tricked him into giving you his silver sword and ten bags of gold."

"We still don't know how you pulled that one off."

"Then you slipped him a sleeping draught that made him snore so that the door joggled and the roof shook and nobody never heard the like, then or now."

"You met me in the mill when the black cat mewled, and lay with me in the moonlight on the tow sacks of meal our daddy had ground by day."

"Then you lay with *me* on the same tow sacks when the old owl hooted three times in the sweet gum tree."

Jack tasted a whiff of the bad liquor he had drunk. He felt another stirring, not of loin but of remorse. The feeling was unfamiliar, and he did not care for it. What was wrong with him? If the three of them managed to get away from this dog why couldn't he lie with them again? He was Jack, after all, *that* Jack. But instead he swallowed. He said, "Forgive me, but I'm not..."

"...Sure you remember us?"

"I—I'm sorry, no, I..." He leaned forward and looked intently into the eyes of one girl and then the eyes of the other.

"They're not limpid pools of amber, Jack," said the first.

"They're light brown."

"And they're not shining or flashing or burning with passion."

"They're just eyes."

Jack glanced back and forth between their lovely faces with increasing consternation. Why couldn't he remember?

"It's just as well you don't recollect us."

"We were fifteen, Jack. *Fifteen.*"

"I know," he said. "I mean, were you? I mean, I guess I know that now because you just told me."

The girls stared at him, their brows slowly lowering.

"It was wrong, what happened," he said, "wasn't it?"

"It was wrong, Jack."

"It was wrong before you even stepped forward into that particular setting out."

The liquor roiled in Jack's stomach. Inside his head he felt himself stepping off down an unfamiliar road. No good lay at its end. The way was dark and cold and he was alone and growing older with each step. He couldn't find his shoes. Jagged stones bruised and cut his feet.

"What happened after I left?" he asked, his voice falling so that he could barely hear it. "Tell me what happened next."

One girl blinked into a frown. "Why, nothing happened, Jack. You took the narrator with you. Daddy never woke up from the sleeping draught you gave him. He kept snoring so the door joggled and the roof shook and nobody never heard the like. Except us. We were the only people about the settlement once you left. Eventually the mill rotted down and the dam gave way and the great wheel tipped and toppled into the ivy, where it lays till this day."

"But what happened to *you?*" Jack whispered.

"Me? I just sat by the side of the road weaving a basket of golden straw for to take eggs to the market."

"And *I* sat in the doorway churning a bait of butter for to bake a cake."

"And nobody else came down the road."

"Not ever."

"For ages and ages."

"Till the day I looked up and saw a big black dog a-standin' on the hilltop. At first I was thrilled with joy because we'd been sitting there a hundred years waiting for a new story, and his appearance set us free, but then I realized he meant us no good so I grabbed up my sister and off we ran down the road."

"And after an age and a day of running down the road and over the creek and fighting through the corn, here we are," the other girl said, sweeping her arm around the wheat field. "Here we are. We found you, and we found us a narrator."

Jack looked nervously over his shoulder. A few more girls, stragglers, splashed out of the corn. They looked haggard, their simple country dresses soiled and torn. They hurdled by beat and bored and glared at him as they passed. He saw in their eyes that they recognized him, but nobody smiled and nobody waved and nobody stopped. Nobody asked for his help. He forgot to look at their fair nether parts as they ran away. Jack turned to the twins.

He said, "All these girls, I—"

"Yep."

"Some of 'em twice."

"Are any of 'em, well, you know...?"

"You'd have to ask them."

"Are you proud of yourself, Jack?"

"That's what we want to know, Jack that Jack. Tell us, are you proud?"

Jack was ashamed of what he had done—maybe for the first time in his life—but still, in his most secret heart, he wished that he had counted as the girls ran away. "Well," he admitted. "Maybe a mite."

"Then what are their names?" demanded one.

"Names?" Jack said.

"You heard her. Their names."

Jack realized he had never known any of their names. They had all been farmers' daughters and millers' daughters and kings' daughters.

"Uh," he said, thinking hard. "Susan?"

"No, Jack. None of us never *got* names."

"The same way none of us never got more than the one white dress to wear, and it too tight, not even after you saw to it we needed a different color."

"You never saw fit to ask us."

"Not even after you lay with us."

Jack remembered then—as clearly as if he were there—the rhythmic screech of a turning wheel, a dagger of hard moonlight, a girl lying back on a stack of sacked cornmeal, her white dress pushed above her waist. She said, I don't know, Jack. I don't know. But what had that meant, the "I don't know"? He dug the heels of his hands into his eyes. What he wanted most right then was to forget that he had ever set foot in that mill, that he had ever set out down the road that led to that mill, but he could smell the corn dust, hear the wheel, the water, a soft gasp of breath.

"You have put thoughts in my head I find troublesome," Jack said. "Please make it stop."

"It ain't gonna stop, Jack."

"You drank the seeing juice."

"The what?"

"The seeing juice. You drank it all up."

"Out of the jar we put in the road."

"That's why you can see in the dark."

"Oh, no!" Jack wailed. "I shoulda known. Y'all are witches. I thought all the witches was gone! Y'all done went and gave me a potion!"

"We're not witches, Jack. And not maidens. We're just girls."

"We got the seeing juice from the old man beside the road. He said it was something you needed."

"What prodigious perfidy!" Jack said.

"We put out it in the middle of the road so you would find it on your setting out."

"But why?" Jack said. "Why would you do that to me?" But he knew even as he asked the question that its answer was obvious.

"Because we wanted you to see."

"So you would know."

"And now you see."

"And now you know."

"But I don't want to see," Jack said. "And I don't want to know. I just want to set out. I want the sky to be new and the wind fresh on my cheek. I want to feel the warm red dust scrouging up between my toes. I want to whistle off down the road with the lunch my mama made slung over a pole and meet an old man who'll say, 'Howdy, Jack. Today you're going to meet a giant with two heads, here's two silver hatchets.'"

"That ain't going to happen no more, Jack."

"The black dog is going to get us all. He's eating all the stories up from the inside."

"So enjoy it while you can."

"It's almost like living, this knowing."

Jack grabbed the twins by their hands and tried to pull them with him through the wheat.

"It's no use, Jack. Just let us go."

"No," Jack said, squeezing their hands so tightly he was afraid he might hurt them. "I ain't gonna turn you loose."

"It's fine like this, Jack," said one. "It's fine."

"It's not fine," he said.

"We're lucky in a way," said the other. "We got to be in another story. Even if it was with you."

"We're not weaving baskets and churning butter when nobody never comes. This is better."

"But the way it ends. . . ." Jack said.

"Is the way it ends. The black dog's gonna catch us and say what it is he has to say and he'll bite us and we'll scream and that'll be that."

"Come with me," Jack pleaded, not knowing if their coming with him was even a narrative option. He had always traveled alone. "I'll get us a farm. How about that? I'll get us a farm and clear some new ground and sow some seeds and grow some corn and a few tomatoes and I won't set out no more. I won't be in any more stories. I'll try to be a regular man. Come with me and I'll marry one of you and won't lay a finger on the other one, I promise. We can grow us up a barnload of kids and live happily ever after."

"Oh, Jack," one chided. "You don't *do* happily ever after."

"I do, too," protested Jack. "I've done happily ever after lots of times."

"But then the page turns."

"The page turns and off you go again."

"Shut *up,*" Jack said. "Just shut *up* and come *on.*"

He tried to jerk the girls after him. Their hands were sweaty, almost hot to the touch, calloused from weaving and churning. When they pulled back against him he squeezed harder and felt their delicate bones rubbing together underneath their skin.

"Ow!" said the girl he clutched with his left hand. "You're hurting me!"

"You let her go!" cried the girl on his right just as she clouted him upside the head. "Don't you hurt her no more!"

Jack dropped the hands of both girls and rubbed his ringing ear. He said, "What the hell'd you do that for? I'm just trying to save you!" But when he looked up the girls were gone, just gone, vanished as completely as if they had been imagined along the side of a road, and just as quickly forgotten.

Across the oceanic distance ahead of Jack lay the brushstroke of tree line in which he might conceivably find shelter from the black dog, while behind him rose the porous dam of tasseled corn through which the dog might at any moment break. To either side vast calms of wheat promised neither near-horizon nor hope. Jack turned again through the compass points, this way, then that way, but reckoned only despair. The cornfield lay too close behind him, the forest too far ahead. And as a child of the mountains his aversion to blank horizons was inbred and inalienable. Jack thought, How bleak a vista viewed from the doldrums of squandered life! Then he spat disgustedly because, as a plot man, he distrusted metaphor.

He took a heavy step toward the distant smudge of forest, stopped, shook his head and considered weeping. Who needed maidens anyway? Bedding a maiden was a lot of work. He took another step, then another and another until he creaked into an arthritic lumber. Maybe from now on he would concentrate on widows. Widows didn't smell as good as maidens, but they needed less convincing. The thought gave him resolve enough to ramp up into a run. He had no desire to run but ran nonetheless, getting on with his setting out because he was Jack, *that* Jack, and that was what he did—he set out—and that was all he knew, or had ever known, to do. He had never set down in any one place. Despite what he'd told the twins, he didn't even know if such a thing was possible. The implications hurt Jack's brain. Until the girls tricked him into drinking the seeing juice he had never been one to snag his jacket in the thicket of existential thought.

But what *if* he had hunkered down in some green valley and let the narrator go off down the road without him? Could he have lived the life of a regular man? Or was what the dog said true? If he stopped moving would he simply cease to be? He had sauntered carelessly through the stories, had taken for granted that another tale lay beyond the one through which he passed. How many times had Mama packed him a bite of dinner and kissed him good-bye at the gate? How many dew-tamped, red dirt roads had unrolled before him in the sweet of the morning? What *would* it have been like if he had stayed put and settled down with any one of the maidens who had inexplicably loved him, or had at least loved the charming but insincere version of himself he had conjured without scruple? The dog would never have had reason to run him to ground. Day stacking upon numbered day would have gently done the dog's work. At the end of his life he would have faded into memory and anecdote, a regular man, slipping away for good on the last breath that uttered his name.

And would that have been such a bad thing? Waking with the same woman beside him for a finite number of mornings, breathing in her familiar smell? Watching a yardful of children chase lightning bugs in the cool of the evening? Having a boy named Little Jack follow you down the road when you set out, then home when you turned around? Could he find in such small things satisfactory treasure? He didn't know if he would ever be presented the chance to clamber onto the precious, puny arc of a mortal life, or even if he would do so should the chance present itself, but he did not want to die alone in this foul folktale, in a conclusion not of his choosing, so he kept on, dog be damned.

Jack ran for miles and empty miles, his mind free from the embarrassment of exposition, the regret of flashback, the dread of foreshadow, beneath a dawning, electrical sky tinted the bilious gray of nausea. Pink sears of lightning intermittently scratched across it, followed by ripped barks of thunder.

The close air occasionally rearranged itself as if uncomfortable, worrying the wheat into restive eddies, but this humid stirring brought with it no relief, only the promise of storm. He ran until he noticed with a waking start that the forest toward which he traveled had grown markedly closer, that it was now serrated by individual treetops. A single tree, an oak of considerable height, elevated on a plinth of some sort, had separated itself from the forest, well forward of the phalanx. Jack looked nervously behind him for the dog before slowing to a trot as he approached. The tree's position at the forefront of the cohort suggested it was a tree of some importance, a sentinel at least, maybe a general or a king of the trees; Jack guessed it was also probably a talking tree, given its perch on a pulpit. He had encountered only a few talking trees during his journeys, and for the most part found them to be on the dull side, so limited in their experience of the world. In their low, sapped voices they talked torpidly about the circling seasons, the glacial ripple of their growth rings.

Jack checked over his shoulder again and pulled up into a walk. Whatever the tree's rank he figured it was a tree he should howdy to before he piled into the woods.

"Hello, Daddy!" he called.

No answer.

He searched among its limbs and leaves for some sign of sentience. He wondered, as he often had, why some trees talked and some didn't. And how could you tell the difference between a tree that couldn't talk, and a tree that could talk but chose not to?

When he stopped near the tree he saw that it wasn't perched on top of a platform after all, but, rather, grew from the center of a moldering boat. Well, Jack thought, standing with his hands on his hips, his hat pushed back, a boat. He stared and stared, unable to stop staring, not so much at the incongruity of a boat locked in a vast waste of wheat, trackless miles from the sea, but with the rising recognition, as cold in his gut as a gulp of water from a winter spring, that he knew this boat from somewhere, that it was (or at least had been) a magic boat, a flying boat, and that he had flown in it. He had sailed, he remembered now, over the dogwood-splatted mountains and green fields striped with furrows, surrounded by friends he hadn't yet betrayed, all of them whooping with joy because they were young and it was spring and the fresh sun and rushing wind were warm on their faces and they were, of all things, flying in a boat. The boat rotting before him, its hull split by a tree, had once been his boat.

The old man had given Jack the boat because Jack, occasionally generous in those days, had shared his simple lunch of ashcake with the stranger. (Jack's good-for-nothing older brothers, Will and Tom, passing that way before Jack, had refused to share their fancy victuals with the old man. And for their stinginess no good came to that pair!) When Jack had called "Sail, Boat, Sail!" the boat had risen into the air and careered through the sky. He held tight to the gunnels and navigated by whim. When he said "Sail Over Here!" the boat sailed over here, and when he said "Sail Over There!" it sailed over there. He picked up Hardy Hardhead and Eatwell and

Drinkwell and Seewell and Shootwell and Hearwell and Runwell, all those boys, and they flew hooting through the sky to the king's house, where they tricked the witch who had spelled the king's daughter out of all her gold, breaking the maiden's enchantment in the process. He remembered with a slap of regret that he had then married the king's daughter but left her for another tale shortly after their honeymoon. He wondered now why he had done that. She had loved him. Her breath had tasted like a waft of iris; her breasts had fit his hands like apples. Nor did he share the gold he had gotten with the Well boys, although without them he could never have beaten the witch. Instead he had swiped a pan of cold biscuits and a jug of wine out of the king's kitchen, slung the gold sack over his shoulder, and set off whistling down the starlit road.

The boat was in a sorry state. Jack knelt beside it now and scooped out mud and moldy leaves and acorns and bits of stick with his hands, finding that the keel had mostly blighted into earth. The tree had sprouted in the muck and grown to full measure, pushing up planking with its roots as it grew. Jack sat back on his haunches and considered whether it was possible to get the boat airborne again. "Fix, Boat, Fix," he commanded, but it remained as rotten and unmoving as before. He also tried "Mend, Boat, Mend" and "Repair, Boat, Repair" and even the evangelical "Heal, Boat, Heal!" to no avail. He stepped over the gunnel into the boat and with his foot tested the bench in the stern from which he had so blithely navigated the sky. Convinced the seat would bear his weight, Jack sat and rested his chin in his hand, beneath the wide canopy of the tree, and gazed without seeing at the oak's knobby hide.

The night he had sneaked away from the king's daughter and stiffed the Well boys he had simply walked off down the road. Why hadn't he at least taken the boat? If he was going to set out anyway wouldn't that have made more sense? He could have sailed through the rest of the tales, Jack and His Flying Boat! The miles liquid in his wake! Oh, the giants he could have killed! The sacks of gold he could have snagged! And the maidens—well, the maidens, he thought shamefully—who knew what pleasures he could've made with a maiden in a flying boat? Instead he had left the boat moored in the king's yard when he sneaked away. It must have flown off on its own, pilotless, adrift in the sky, searching for him, its lost Captain Jack, before marooning itself who knew how many years ago in this damnable field. When he mumbled "Sail, Boat, Sail" he already knew it wasn't going to work.

A breeze bearing the salted singe of ozone puffed onto Jack's cheek. Above him the oak leaves had begun to curl against coming weather, their pale undersides furled in warning. In the direction from which Jack had run a great dark cloud hoisted above the far horizon, its roiling mass black as blindness, its towering edges limned with mercurial silver. Detonations of lightning flared inside the cloud, followed by broadsides of thunder. Between the cloud's trailing edge and the ground lay a sickly stripe of greenish sky, and silhouetted against the sky galloped a solitary figure.

Jack, cursing himself for his interlude of aeronautical nostalgia, leapt to his feet preparatory to lighting out, but saw that the figure running toward him was a man, not the black dog. Jack skimmed through the possibilities of who the man might be: the farmer whose whoring wife he had attempted to mount the evening before had seemed content to run him off, not run him down; it had been so long since he had defiled a maiden that he couldn't imagine an avenging daddy would still be on his trail; and surely all the millers and kings and robbers and giants he had tricked out of their gold would have given up all hope of restitution and retribution by now. Maybe, Jack thought, just maybe it was the old man, bearing magic words and implements, come to save him. Howdy, Daddy, Jack would say, come on up in my boat and sit a spell. Why thank you, the old man would answer, I believe I will. Jack would do the old man a small kindness—maybe give him a dollar—and by the time the old man had taken leave of the tale, he would have either repaired Jack's boat, or given Jack the wherewithal to kill the dog. Jack eased back onto the bench, fighting the urge to head for the woods, reminding himself that he had never feared a regular man.

The man stopped about fifty yards away and stared in the direction of Jack and his boat, his head cocked thoughtfully to one side. "Jack?" the man asked as he edged closer a slow step at a time. "Is that you?"

"Why, Tom Dooley," Jack said. "I wouldn't have thought about you for a hundred dollars."

For coming up on a hundred and fifty years, the fans of

Jack and the fans of Tom Dooley had fought over which man was rightful heir of the high kingship of Appalachian folklore. Jack's proponents denounced Tom Dooley with his lone ballad as a one-hit wonder, while the Dooleyists maintained that the *real* Jack was Jack's English forebear, famous climber of the bean*stalk,* and not this Jack here, stalker of the southern highlands, climber of the dialectical bean*tree.* Although neither Jack nor Tom Dooley would ever admit it, each of the assertions hit a nerve with one or the other: Jack was secretly sensitive that his renown, while considerable, was almost entirely regional; Tom Dooley silently suffered because, despite his greater success farther afield, he was summoned in only a solitary song. They had never been formally introduced, but had often glared at each other across auditoriums and coffeehouses. Both their crowds, oddly enough, seemed to run in the same pack.

Tom Dooley hung down his head. "Look here, Jack, to be honest with you, I don't feel much like feuding today. Can we put it in a poke for now?"

Jack exhaled, relieved. "That seems fair enough."

Tom Dooley scratched his chin and considered the tree spread over Jack's boat. "Jack, ain't that tree you're sitting under a *Quercus alba?*"

Jack picked up a leaf and studied it. "Yep. *Quercus alba.*"

"Shoot, I was hoping it was a *Quercus rubra.* Ordinarily I try to avoid white oaks."

"I don't blame you," Jack said, "but since this one ain't down in some lonesome valley, it's probably all right."

Tom Dooley considered some more. "That boat you're sitting in, ain't it the flying boat where you picked up Hardy Hardhead and the Well boys and went and beat the witch out of all her gold and broke the enchantment the witch put on the king's daughter?"

"It is, but I don't think it flies no more."

"I always liked that story," Tom Dooley said. Then he winced and swallowed and looked at the ground, so painful the admission that he admired anything having to do with Jack.

Jack stared up into the leaves of the tree and drew a deep breath. "And I always liked that knife / life couplet in your ballad. The word 'knife' sounds sharp, like it'd cut you if you drew your finger across it. It makes sense you could use a knife to take a life."

"Why, thank you, Jack. I always thought that rhyme made the song."

Neither man spoke for a stiff moment.

"You doing any good with the song?" Jack finally asked.

"Oh, just middlin'," Tom Dooley said. "A little Girl Scout action, that's about it. Occasional old hippie frailing a banjo. To be honest, I ain't done much good since Burl Ives died. Jack tales doing all right?"

Jack made a face. "Ah, storytelling festivals, mostly. Appalachian Studies scholar every once in a while, but the pointy-heads have done drunk that well about dry."

"Law, law," Tom Dooley sighed. "What a world."

"I know it," Jack said. "Don't I know it."

"Jack?"

"Yeah?"

"Can I get up in that magic boat with you and sit a spell?"

"I don't think it's magic anymore, but you're welcome."

All the benches other than the one on which Jack sat had rotted into collapse or been shoved askew by the growing tree. Jack scooted to one side and Tom Dooley sat down beside him. Jack cast a weather eye on the approaching cloud. It had grown so tall he had to tilt his head back to see its anvil top. Shreds of updraft steamed continuously along its black sides. He hated to leave his boat again after all these years but figured that it would soon be in his best interest to head for the woods. Whatever mayhem that storm was packing, Jack didn't want to be caught out in it. In the forest he might find suitable shelter. A robbers' cabin would be good. The robbers were never at home in the stories, but the wife of the leader always was. The wife tended to be lonely and he often talked her out of a little slice before she hid him in her hope chest when they heard the gang coming back with their spoils.

"Jack?" Tom Dooley said. "I need to ask you something else. Is today tomorrow?"

"Hmm," Jack said. "It was yesterday."

"I was afraid of that. See, my song's always been mostly in the future present tense. You know how it goes, "Come this time *tomorrow,* that's when I'm supposed to be hanging from the white oak tree down in the lonesome valley."

"So? If today is today, then tomorrow's still going to be tomorrow, so you're all right."

"But I took off running *yesterday,* Jack, and I run all night, which I have never done before because it ain't in the song, and when it got first light this morning I said, Oh shit, Tom Dooley, you just run plumb out of yesterday and into tomorrow and now you're in a world of trouble."

"That's an interesting temporal conundrum," Jack said.

"Tell me about it. You ain't going to believe this, Jack, but I'm being pursued by a talking dog that maintains he's going to kill me because I've lost cultural currency."

"We're in the same boat, there," Jack said.

"He's after you, too?"

"Got after me last night."

"I'll be damned," Tom Dooley said.

In the far distance the wheat began to thrash away from Jack and Tom Dooley, almost parallel to the ground, sucked toward the cloud by some virulent rip, while the leaves clinging to the topmost branches of the white oak still shivered away from them on a high breeze Jack could not feel in the boat.

"Tom Dooley, we better move on out," Jack said. "I fear this gathering cumulonimbus bears us ill will."

"How about you try the boat again?"

"Sail, Boat, Sail!"

Nothing.

"Maybe if we got out and rocked it back and forth a little bit," Tom Dooley said, "tried to prize it loose from the dirt."

"Alas, the boat I fear / Shall fly no more / Its magic run aground / In this landlock of grain," spoke an ancient voice whose component parts seemed to flutter down around them.

"Day Lord have mercy, Jack!" Tom Dooley said. "It's a talking tree! It liked to have started me to death." He craned his neck and squinted into the canopy. "Why does it talk like that?"

"In the sacred timbre / Of my ancestors / I speak," the tree said.

"Oh, cut it out," Jack said. "This is North Carolina. We're prose people."

"Ah, sweet Carolina! / With your virgin soil / Grasp me by my taproot."

"Was that dirty?" Tom Dooley asked.

"Come on," Jack said. "This pretentious prosody weighs heavy on my person. We need to move on out of here before the storm or the black dog one gets us." He stood and started to step out of the boat.

"Wait!" the tree cried in panicked prose. "You're Jack, *that* Jack. I'm the last of the talking trees, and the black dog has promised to raise its leg against me! What should I do? Where should I fly?"

"What did you just say?" Tom Dooley said.

The tree didn't answer, but a flail of leaves rattled down among them.

"Jack, the damn tree's holding out on us!" Tom Dooley cried. "Your boat can still fly!" He stood and from somewhere in his overalls produced a bloodstained butcher knife of priapic length. "You listen here, stovewood. I swear on Laurie Foster's lonesome grave that if you don't make this boat fly I will carve hearts and obscenities all over your worthless trunk."

"All right, all right!" the tree said. "Put that thing away before somebody gets whittled. The truth is, once I took root I began to absorb the magic that leached out of the boat as it rotted away. I don't know if I can make it fly or not. I've never tried. Trees are naturally averse to flying."

"Why you deciduous son of a bitch," Jack said. "You broke my boat."

"The boat was rotten when the squirrel buried my nut! You can't blame me for your toxic waste!"

"If I still had my silver ax..."

"Hey, Jack?" Tom Dooley said.

"I wonder how many two by tens I can get out of you?" Jack snarled.

"Jack—" Tom Dooley interrupted.

"What?"

"There's a posse coming yonder."

From beneath the storm cloud a countless multitude of men on horseback pounded toward the boat, guns drawn, long dusters flapping out behind them like black wings. Bright whips of lightning cracked all around them. Hounds whose stiff tails cut periscopic wakes through the wheat loped among the horses; their trailing bays melded into a single cyclonic moan.

"Why so many of 'em?" Tom Dooley marveled.

"Every time someone sings that song of yours a lawman sets out on your trail with a brace of hounds," the tree said.

"God Almighty," Tom Dooley said. "Look how famous I am!"

"Look how famous I am," Jack simpered. "Well, you ought to have seen the crowd of maidens I diddled run through here this morning."

The hoofbeats of the horses thrummed faintly into earshot, intermittently drowned out by fusillades of thunder. The sounding of the hounds rose in pitch and ardor and the lawmen raised their weapons. Shreds of gun smoke ghosted silently from the barrels of their pistols, followed moments later by almost inaudible pops. Bullets dropped softly into the wheat between the riders and the boat, along with the first frigid splats of rain. The throbbing of the hooves grew louder. Beneath Jack's feet the ground buzzed with their drumming.

"Okay, I've enjoyed my renown enough for one day," Tom Dooley said. "We need to head on down the road."

"Let's see what you got, tree," Jack said. "Them posse boys are coming for us all."

The tree cleared its throat, wherever that was. "O ancient gods of earth, wind, and fire, gods of sky and cloud and rain, gods of leaf and blossom and bole, gods of light and dark and season—"

"Oh, good Lord," Jack said. "We ain't got time for this pseudo-religious New Age nickering."

"Be respectful, Jack," Tom Dooley whispered. "The tree's pantheistic."

"—summon from my reaching roots the magic once contained in this vessel's enchanted planking and lift us into the darkening sky! Save us from the black dog! From the approaching posse! From the lightning and wind and storm! In the name of the sacred buzzing bee, MAKE US FLY!"

Jack and Tom Dooley sat very still.

"Well?" Jack asked.

"Wait a second," the tree said. "Okay. Try it now."

"Sail, Boat, Sail," Jack commanded.

For a moment nothing happened, but then, for yards around the boat, the tree's roots tore themselves free from the ground with a great ripping noise. Clod-spewing waves of root rolled toward the base of the tree and the boat bucked in the ensuing collision.

"Son of a squirrel," the tree groaned. "That hurt like a woodpecker."

A handful of bullets from the approaching riders snipped almost delicately through the tree's leaves, and a salvo of thunder ignited above them. Tom Dooley ducked and laced his fingers above his head as he attempted to hide beneath his hat. The tree flopped back and forth with a clatter of branches and leaves as it struggled to pull its anchoring taproot free. "Say it, Jack!" the tree grunted. "Say it again!"

"Sail, Boat, Sail! Sail, Boat, Sail!"

The cloud had moved almost directly above their heads, thinning the light around them into near darkness. A roaring curtain of rain dropped from the sky and slid toward them across the field. From inside the deluge the baying of the hounds approached hysteria and clamored into a frenetic yipping.

The closing riders shouted in vicious paraphrase, *"Tom Dooley! Tom Dooley! Your head! Hang it down!"*

The boat trembled beneath Jack. "SAIL, BOAT, SAIL!" he screamed.

"Tom Dooley!" taunted the lawmen. *"Guess what you're bound to do!"*

"Go, go, go," Tom Dooley prayed. "Go, go, go."

As the taproot rent from the ground the vessel shuddered into the air a ripping inch at a time. Most of the rotted planking in the bottom of the hull peeled away as the boat rose. Jack and Tom Dooley grabbed hold of the bench and lifted their feet. When the root broke free with a final snap the boat floated into the sky as lightly as dandelion down. It rose as high as a house, a barn, a tree, a standard-sized giant, a two-headed giant, a three-headed giant, two trees. They rose as high as a mountain, as two mountains. At three mountains high the boat banked gracefully toward the woods; its bow tipped urgently forward as it shot away from the swirling maw of the cloud, its roots swimming aft like tentacles, leaving a silver contrail of leaves spinning in its wake. Within moments it crossed the boundary of the forest, sailing for far shores. The leading line of lawmen pulled up at the crater that remained where the tree had stood and gazed after the boat, their faces pallid beneath the wide brims of their dripping black hats. The hounds cast about the trampled wheat in confusion, as if they had made some mistake in their trailing. Jack looked for the black dog but did not see him in the rain. Not one of the watching lawmen thought to shoot at the boat as it grew smaller in the distance. Looking back, Jack glimpsed the full magnitude of the peace officers come to lay Tom Dooley in his grave. A slick of riders and dogs blackened the field as far as he could see. Millions.

"We're flying, Jack!" Tom Dooley yelled. "We're flying!"

Jack's joy at once again sailing through the air in his boat was tempered in almost equal part by his wish that the boat were still intact. He wasn't afraid of heights—he was a jim-dandy beantree climber, after all—but found that flying at great speed in a boat without a bottom, while exhilarating, made for a vexatious voyage. He gripped the gunnel so tightly that when his Saturday hat blew off he didn't even try to grab it. At last he allowed himself to look down past his dangling shoes and through the writhe of roots. A topography of trees blurred beneath them. As he watched the forest passing he realized that the posse wouldn't be able to follow them through such verdant woods on horseback. The lawmen would have to dismount and send for lumberjacks and that would take time. He had gotten away! He was *still* Jack, that, by God, Jack! He let go of the gunnel first with his left hand, then the right, and placed his hands on his knees. He couldn't see forward because of the tree trunk (and didn't think to look aft, where the storm still avidly pursued them), but he reckoned that, for now, seeing where he was going didn't matter as much as the fact that he was gone. He was once again flying in a magic boat. The whole world and its riches lay ahead of him. He thrust his arms into the air. "Woo-hoo!" he hollered. "Woo-hoo!"

He wrapped his arm around Tom Dooley's shoulder and gave him a shake. "Where to, Daddy?" he asked. "Where do you want to go?"

"Why, I don't know, Jack."

"How about we pick up a couple of maidens, you and me, get a bite to eat, see the sights?" He had forgotten, for the moment, his recent maiden-related resolutions. "How about we get you a girl up here in my flying boat?"

"Better not," Tom Dooley said. "I'd just wind up sticking a knife in her chest and burying her in the woods."

When Jack removed his arm from Tom Dooley's shoulders, he drew back a long string of blue sparks along with it. He felt as if the air around him were being inhaled. His blowing hair cackled with static.

Tom Dooley turned to him and said, "Jack?" just as the sky blew up.

A white scald of light blinded Jack; a cannon shot of sound deafened him; the rivets on his overalls branded him, and fire shot from the nails of his boots. For a heartbeat he gazed at a blank page in a book and wondered what happened next. Then he smelled wood smoke and opened his eyes. He found he was clinging to the starboard gunnel with both arms, his legs waving beneath him. The boat rotated slowly—first this way, then that—as it slipped from the sky. The tree's trunk was split and scorched and smoking all the way down to its base; its canopy unraveled in a corkscrew of blackened leaf scrap as it fell. Tom Dooley was fighting to keep hold of the snarl of roots beneath the boat.

"JAAACK!" Tom Dooley yelled.

Jack swung a leg up and clambered back into the boat. He was considerably singed, but nothing seemed to be burned off.

"JAAACK! HELP!"

"Sail, Boat, Sail, Sail, Boat, Sail, Sail, Boat, Sail," Jack begged.

Nothing. The boat began to pendulum as it stalled toward the woods far below. The wind rushing past Jack's ears roared with fervor.

"The boat's not working, Tom Dooley!" Jack called. "Hang on! We're going down!"

Tom Dooley managed to claw his way up into a root snarl near the base of the trunk. "Tell the tree to say a sestina or something! He's the one sucked up all the magic!"

"The tree's dead, Tom Dooley! It took a direct hit. There's sap all over the place."

"Not dead," the tree rasped, "but cleaved."

"You're alive!" Jack cried.

"Charcoal, Jack. I'll be briquettes soon enough."

"No! Wait wait wait wait wait wait! Listen. We're in a bad way here. We're going down. We're going to crash. Tell us what to do. Tree! Hang on long enough to tell us what to do!"

"Taproot," it rasped. "The magic's leaking from my taproot."

"I see it!" Tom Dooley yelled. "Law, law, Jack. The damn thing's shitting rubies!"

"*Bleeding* rubies," the tree said.

"*Rubies?*" Jack asked.

"Magic in its solid form. Ordinarily it's a gas."

"Magic rubies," Tom Dooley wondered out loud. "Damn, Jack, this here is some more kind of story."

"Can you stop the leak?" Jack asked him.

"I think so!" Tom Dooley said.

He hung upside down trapeze-style and jammed his finger into the hole.

"Ow!" the tree yelped. "Take it easy down there!"

"Sorry!" Tom Dooley called.

The oak's rocking slowed and stilled. The bow tipped up and settled. The boat came to a full stop and floated becalmed in the air.

"It worked, Tom Dooley!" Jack shouted. "By God, it worked! We're not falling anymore!"

"Huzzah!" Tom Dooley shouted anachronistically.

It was not long, however, until their deliverance from death began to strike them as more plight than providence. Although the boat hovered easily, it proved incapable of progress. When Jack commanded it to "Sail Over Here!" it did not respond; when he ordered it to "Sail Over There!" it remained anchored in place. The cloud slid blackly by mere yards above their heads and tried to beat them from the sky with head-knocking hailstones and icy cataracts of rain. It lit up on the inside as if some haint with a lantern were seeking them through its dark passageways, opening doors and peering inside rooms in which they might be hiding. The earth below them had disappeared beneath the deluge. Jack shielded his noggin with his forearms and shivered mightily; he had never been so cold—or so frightened—in all his many travels. The tree could offer neither comfort nor counsel as its condition worsened; scores of leaves leapt into the rain as its consciousness wavered. When the end came only a few lifeless stragglers flapped from its boughs, ragged flags among the rigging of a ghost ship.

"I think that I shall never see," the tree whispered, then spoke no more.

After the tree died Tom Dooley grew broody and silent. "Jack?" he finally said. "I'm getting a cramp in my finger, and all the blood's run to my head."

"I reckon that would be the case, given your predicament."

"And you know what I just realized? I'm hanging from a white oak tree, just like I say I'm gonna be doing tomorrow, in the first-person part of my song."

"I hadn't thought about it, but I guess that's right," Jack said. "Spirit of the ballad, anyway, if not exactly the letter."

"I never been in a tomorrow before, and when I finally get to one I wind up hanging from a daggum white oak tree. It's been interesting, though—the talking dog and the talking tree and the flying boat and getting struck by lightning and the magic rubies leaking out. To tell you the truth, I've always envied you living inside a story instead of a song. Not knowing what happens on the next page, all that setting out, going on down the road, seeing what happens the other side of the mountain."

"I've had some good times, I guess," Jack said. "You don't like living in your song?"

"It sucked the soul out of me a long time ago. It's always the same. Even when I close my eyes I can hear that refrain a-comin'. I got to where I looked forward to somebody screwing up the lyrics just for a change, but they're so damn simple hardly anybody ever did. Today's the most improvisation I ever been involved in."

"I'm sorry about that," Jack said. "The limitations of the lyric. At least you're out now."

"I don't know about that, Jack. I just realized my head's hanging down, just like it says in the chorus."

Jack sat up straighter. "Hey now," he said. "That's just happenstance. It's the only way you could stop the rubies leaking and the boat from crashing."

"It's not happenstance, neither, Jack. It's prescient, is what it is. Even after all I been through since yesterday I'm still locked up in the song. Head hanging down. Hanging from a white oak tree. The whole pokeful. It's the damnedest thing. Narrative inevitability."

Jack glared down at the bottoms of Tom Dooley's shoes. "You ain't locked up in shit," he said. "Ain't nothing inevitable. That ain't how a story works. You get to a hard spot you make a decision and you set out from there. You go on down the road and you see what happens next. Then you make another decision. You got *agency.*"

"But I ain't got agency. It's all an illusion. Face facts."

"Them ain't my facts."

"I come this far, Jack, I might as well go on back to my ballad. I know it ain't much of a song, but if I'm bound to die

I'd just as soon do it on the home ground. If my words get all the way forgot, well, then that's all right. You seen all them lawmen riding after me through the wheat field. I been sung about more than most."

"That's chickenshit rationalization, Tom Dooley. If that's the way you think, I don't know why you even bothered running from that dog."

Tom Dooley bent forward and moved a tangle of roots out of the way and blinked up at Jack through the rain. "Why, Jack," he said. "Ain't nobody likes getting bit by a dog."

"Tom Dooley, if you pull your finger out of that hole, we can't go back. We'll both die and I flat don't care to. I ain't never been killed before, in all these many stories, and I don't aim to start now."

"Well, I'm *bound* to die, Jack. I don't know about you." And with that he pulled his finger out of the hole and shook out his arm.

Jack saw a ruby bob out from beneath the tree and hover in the air. Magic. The boat shivered ever so slightly.

"Why, you son of a bitch," he said.

"Hey, Jack," Tom Dooley said, glaring up, his murderer's eyes blackening with glee. "Come this time tomorrow, reckon where *you'll* be?" Then he laughed, somersaulted backward, and vanished into the rain.

Before Jack finished wondering if Tom Dooley had hit the ground, the taproot belched out a clot of rubies and the boat dropped far enough to yank a holler out of Jack. Without thinking he leapt feet first through the bottom of the boat and on through the root-jumble, hooked his legs on the trapeze root, and jammed his finger into the ruby hole. Although the boat now floated steadily in the squall, he found himself pondering the same predicament that had stymied him while Tom Dooley was the one who stanched the ruby-bleeding: namely, how to get down from the sky. As he hung upside down his head pounded and his feet numbed and his finger throbbed and he shook in the downpour, and when a rogue hailstone caught him in the testy parts, he let loose a malediction of blasphemous execrations worthy of the most degenerate giant. At least the cloud had stopped shooting lightning at him. Just as the idea of ending his own tale with what he now thought of as the Dooley solution flickered in the far darkness of his considering, it occurred to him that he might lower the boat by letting a few rubies at a time drip from the tree. The plan worked well enough but he couldn't grow used to the lurching in his gut each time the boat jerked, even though he knew it was coming. After a while he began to worry that the tree would run out of rubies before the boat lit on the ground, and that he would be squashed into Jack jelly when the tree landed on top of him. Lost as he was in the deluge, unable to gauge or guess at his altitude, he also worried that even if the tree *didn't* run out of rubies he would still be mashed into mush if he didn't see the ground coming up in time. The rubies themselves proved irksome. They didn't fall once squeezed from the tree, but instead floated around Jack's head like a swarm of glittering gnats worth, in his estimation, upward of a bazillion dollars. He tried cramming a handful into the bib pocket of his overalls, so as to sell them later, but had to let them go when he almost floated away. Thus the greatest treasure hunter in the history of the high country was reduced to waving away from his face the greatest gob of gemstones he had ever laid eyes on. If only he could have gotten his feet on the ground with a couple of pocketsful he would have been able to set himself up in the biggest king's castle in the countryside!

Jack had no idea how far the boat had descended, and he had grown almost bored with the process of bleeding the taproot when the last of the magic rubies was birthed from the wounded tree. He stared in disbelief at the hole until he felt the boat falter, then he scrambled out of the root ball and up the tree trunk, squealing like a kindled witch. He wrapped his arms and legs around the tree's biggest limb with no inkling how far he was about to fall. The boat dropped like a golden egg out of a goose but turned out to be only a two-headed giant or so above the ground when it fell. It was also dead-aimed for the roof of a tiny house. Jack had only a second or two to close his eyes and brace for impact. The crash sounded as if the whole valley of Ezekiel's dry bones had broken at once, but the tree remained providentially upright. Jack was none the worse for wear. The boat and tree, however, had smashed the house into a pile of mayhem and midden approaching the smithereen. From his perch in the tree Jack spied in the rubble half a burnt-looking cornbread pone, the intact globe of a kerosene lamp, a disemboweled feather pillow, a Sunday school *Quarterly* wrinkling in the rain, a wrecked wardrobe chomping a pair of overalls, and the lower part of a woman's leg, shod in a worn brogan laced half-way up, sticking out from beneath the brick pile formed by the toppled chimney.

"Hello, the house," he called to the shoe, neither expecting, nor receiving, a reply.

Jack first hoped that the leg and the boot belonged to a robber's wife, which would spot him tolerable time to run away, given that robbers never came home until midnight, some nights as late as one or one thirty. But when he slid down from the tree and squatted beside the boot, he remembered that all the robbers' wives with whom he had lain had been lovely in their loneliness, and that he had never taken any of them away from the hard lives in which he had found them, although many of them had asked. And while he had killed a fair number of regular men over the years, he couldn't recall ever killing a woman who hadn't been a witch. This was new ground he was clearing. His first impulse was to take off before somebody happened by, but setting out seemed simultaneously like a good idea and the worst intention. He thought that saying a few words over the foot might be appropriate, but he had never learned any of those words. He poked the sole of the boot with his forefinger. He pinched the first little piggy and wiggled the foot back and forth. Finally he whispered, "Sorry to bother you, ma'am," then stood and turned and picked his way through the wreckage, forlorn and baffled. Although killing the woman hadn't been his fault exactly, he was starting to believe the maidens in the wheat field had been right about his character, or lack thereof. And it did not, in fact, occur to him to dig the woman out.

Around the house-yard stood a passel of paltry outbuildings peculiar in their decrepitude. Each of them tilted so far toward toppling it seemed miraculous not one of them had fallen over. No two of the hovels canted in the same direction, which made them dizzying to contemplate. The door to the outhouse—the most upright of the shacks—banged open and the old man stomped out into the rain and the mud sop, struggling to pull up and secure his overalls while surveying the shambles.

"Dagnabbit, Jack," he spat. "Can't a feller even loosen his dung bung without you dropping out of the sky in a stricken watercraft and busting up his living-house?"

"Old Man!" Jack cried. "It's you! You're alive! Why, I ain't seen you in forever and half a while."

"No offense," the old man grumbled, "but I'd be a heap better off if you wasn't seeing me now." He walked to the door stoop and surveyed the shock of scrap that had lately been his house. He studied what little remained of the flying boat. He gazed into the top of the dead tree. He considered the fallen chimney. He turned and pointed a long, yellow-nailed finger at Jack. "You have visited carnage upon me," he said. "You have wrecked my real estate and busted up my chifforobe. You have killed my old lady deader'n a plow-tongue. She always said, 'Old Man, mark my words, you will come to regret trusting that Jack rascal with a flying boat,' and now I see that you have proved the poor thing prophetic, bless her heart."

"I'm sorry," Jack said, the words queer and toxic-tasting on his tongue. In the past he had said them only to notch a bit of this or that, usually maiden love-favors. But this time he really was.

The old man blinked in surprise and sniffled. "Why, thank you for the sentiment, Jack. Her biscuits'd bust your tooth out and her cornbread wasn't fit to eat, but she was a good old witch and I loved her."

"Say what, now?" Jack said. "You mean to tell me that long as I've known you, lo these many years, all those times I run into you sitting by the roadside during my settings out, you were married to a witch?"

The old man scowled. "Who else did you think I'd be married to?"

"Not a dadblamed witch!" Jack cried. "You know how I hate a witch! I spent my whole career trying to cull the coven!"

"Then you might as well cull me, too."

Jack grabbed his head and twisted it back and forth. "Oh, naw," he moaned. "Not you. Please tell me you ain't a witch. How could you betray me like that and you the nearest thing to a friend I ever had?"

"Doggone it, Jack, I oughta spell you right now for saying such. Where do you think all them magical implements I give you come from? You can't go down to the crossroads and buy truck like that in the store. I made and spelled *everything* I give to you. You see them sheds falling over empty? They used to be full of conjuring components. I give you everything I *had*.

That dab of seeing juice I sent by the twins was the last of what there was. Hell, when you was just a little feller, I'm the one bartered you the magic beans for that dried-up cow your conniving mama sent you to town to trade, and they was supposed to be my supper. So don't you come up in here and tell me I betrayed you."

"Mama told me there wasn't nothing wrong with that cow!" Jack said.

"Oh, just hush," the old man said. "That was the poorest cow I ever seen. There wasn't enough milk left in that sack to squirt a barn cat and it sitting in the bucket. You always have been too much of an idiot to know you was one."

Jack stepped forward with his fists balled up. "You need to remember who you're talking to," he snarled. "I'm *still* the only giant-killer in this settlement, and I don't need no magic gewgaws to cull out a witch as old as you."

The old man reached into the side pocket of his overalls and produced a hissing copperhead, which he tossed at Jack's face. Jack opened his mouth to scream, but the snake disappeared into the air an inch before it struck him. Still, he beat and whacked his head and the front of his overalls as if the snake had landed around his shoulders; he danced a jerky jig and stared wildly about his feet.

The old man reached again into his pocket. "You want me to peg another one at you?"

Jack shook his head and whimpered unintelligibly.

"Son, you need to remember you ain't no match for any kind of witch, even one as old as me, unless you got some magic on your side. No regular man is. You're just lucky I'm a good witch."

Jack staggered through the sucking mud past the old man, his heart crazed with beating, and melted onto the wet stoop. He had seen his reflection in the copperhead's eye. "That didn't seem like much of a good witch thing to do," he said.

"Well, you had it coming."

Jack conceded the point with a nod.

"To be honest with you," the old man said, "I'm only mostly good. I will eat me a kid every once in a while, but only the bad'uns that sass their mamas and don't say their prayers. Now, the old lady, she had a sweet tooth for virgins and I had to hide her broom come full-moon time. Her people was all bad witches."

"Did I ever run up on any of her people?"

"Let me see. You kilt three of her cousins in that haunted mill just this side of Argyle, and you disfigured one of her great-aunts up by Grandfather Mountain. It was sometimes a source of disharmony between me and the old lady, the nature of my calling."

Jack shook his head. "I don't know how you come to spend all those years and spells and truck helping me when you could've boodled up all the treasure for yourself. You could've been the one diddled the maidens and flummoxed the giants and stole the gold and soared around in the flying boat with Hardy Hardhead and the Well boys. Why, you could've used your magic to make yourself king of the settlement."

"Jack, you ain't going to understand a word of this, but being a king didn't interest me none, and I never developed a taste for treasure. But making sure no harm come to you once you set out? That there made me rich as I ever cared to be."

A nameless cry laddered up the inside of Jack's ribcage toward the light. "But I'm ethically challenged," he said.

"You are that."

"And I never think about nobody but myself."

"You do not."

"I don't deserve a single thing you give me."

"No, sir, not one. You always have been, and continue to be, a most unworthy vessel."

"Then why—"

"Because, honey, that's what makes it count."

Jack ruminated on the stoop about what the old man had said while the old man circled the tree and poked around in the wreckage, picking up and examining this or that—a wooden spoon, a page from a calendar, a handful of yellow shotgun shells. Every so often he absentmindedly pulled a brick off the chimney pile and tossed it aside. Finally he leaned against the tree and stared into space.

"It doesn't make a lick of sense, what you just told me," Jack eventually said.

"That's how it ought to be. Anybody it makes sense to ain't doing it right." The old man held a vegetable grater up to the light and peered through the bottom of it with one eye.

"What are you rooting around for, anyway?"

"Something outta this mess to give you, I reckon."

Jack snorted. "I don't think you owe me anything else, considering."

"You're right. I don't owe you a thing. But now that it's clearing up you're gonna need to set out here pretty soon."

Jack hadn't noticed that the rain had stopped. He stood and stared up at the sky. The cloud still pondered by just above the level of the treetops, but white shreds of it had begun to waft loose and skim away. Water nattered down through the leaves of the laurel on the ridge behind the yard, and dripped from the wood of the balsam firs and oaks and rhododendron fronting the house. Somewhere farther off a creek loosed from its banks uproared through the countryside. Funny, as soon as he realized that the rain had passed, he began to cold-shimmy inside his soused overalls.

"I don't care to set out," Jack said. "This has been one toilsome tale and I am fain to settle. Can't I just light here for a spell?"

" 'Fraid not, Jack. The old woman's people'll be flying in here directly and they're gonna want to eat your liver, and since the storm stopped squalling that black dog is bound to be about. You need to leave this settlement and cross the creek before the water gets up over the bridge."

"What's on the other side of the bridge?"

"Yonder, I reckon." The old man picked up a chamber pot and wrinkled his nose and slung it aside. He hoisted a frying pan by the handle and tested its weight before tossing it after the chamber pot.

"Well. What's in Yonder?"

"I can't witch it out, Jack, to be fair with you. Nobody knows what lies in Yonder. All I can tell you is, it's where you got to go." The old man lifted a soup pot smashed nearly flat and looked at Jack through a jagged hole ripped in its blackened bottom. "The old woman used to boil squirrels in this. Have you ever eat a boiled squirrel?"

"Can't say that I have," Jack said.

"I don't endorse it," the old man said. He dropped the pan onto the rubble at his feet and gave it a kick.

"So what happens if I don't cross the bridge?" Jack asked. "What if I don't go to Yonder? The last time I tried to cross a bridge, all hell broke loose."

"Jack, honey, listen to me. I hate to say it, but you don't matter up in here no more. Your name is almost forgot. If you stay in this settlement, the black dog's gonna run you to ground, and nobody will never hear tell of you again. At least in Yonder there might be a new tale for you to set out in. Surely a character with your qualifications is bound to catch on in some kind of story."

Jack considered the proposition. He was still *that* Jack enough to desire whatever attention he might find setting out in a new settlement, but he wasn't sure he had the courage to cross the bridge. What if worse things happened in the stories over there than the bad things that were happening over here? And worse yet, what if there weren't any tales over there at all?

"You think I might turn into a regular man over there?"

The old man cocked his head and considered Jack for a spell. "Well, that's a thought," he said, "or you could stay a story man and a giant could gobble you in one chomp like you was a hushpuppy. Ain't no telling." The old man picked up and eyeballed a saucepan, then tossed it over his shoulder.

"I'm afraid to go to Yonder," Jack said, surprising himself. It was the first time he had ever said those words out loud.

"Well, you oughta be." The old man pawed into a splintery pile of roofing shakes and extracted a five-gallon wooden bucket that looked as ancient as the old man himself. Its slatted sides were gray and splintery, its rope bail frayed. The old man lifted the bucket triumphantly and grinned. He picked his way out of the wreckage and presented the bucket to Jack. "There you go."

Jack looked down at the pail, then up at the old man. "It's a bucket," he said.

"Well, it's all I got. Just hush and come on." The old man led Jack up through the yard toward the ridge, where behind the last of the empty outbuildings he showed Jack a water pump. "Fill it up."

"Is it magic water?"

"Naw, it's just water. Go on. Pump. All the way to the top, now."

The pump handle screeched each time Jack lifted it, but a staunch stream of water spurted from the pipe nonetheless. Astonishingly, the pail didn't prove porous. When water began to spill over the lip, Jack grabbed up the bucket and put it back down. "Old Man?" he said. "A five-gallon bucket filled with water makes for a portly pail. Do vessels such as this come in a smaller displacement?"

The old man stared at Jack. "No," he said, with clear distaste.

"How about I pour out half this water, and in effect make it a two-and-a-half-gallon bucket? You know, travel-sized."

"Listen at you," the old man said. "These are dark days." He turned and started down the hill.

"It ain't no silver sword, I'll tell you that right now," Jack mumbled to himself. He picked up the bucket and scuffled after the old man. Both men stopped to gaze at the dead tree growing up out of the house rubble.

"Mercy," the old man sighed. "Ain't that a sight?" He continued down the hill toward the woods, but Jack stayed where he was.

"Aw, don't tell me I gotta set out through a forest," Jack whined. "You know nothing good ever happens in a forest. Giants clearing new ground, witches waving the flies off their candy houses, unicorns looking to horn you. And without magic truck to tote I'd have to run like a beagled rabbit."

"Boy, don't make me come up there and throw a snake at you." The old man pointed at a narrow path striking out through the trees. "You'll be all right in these here woods," he said. "Just keep to the trail till you get to the muddy red road."

"The muddy red road?"

"Yes, follow the muddy red road."

"Follow the muddy red road."

"Correct, but let's not say it again," the old man warned. "It might grow tiresome."

Jack gazed down the darkening path. From the distance

came the continuous breathing of water-roar. "I don't want to go down in there," he said.

"I know you don't, honey," the old man said. "But you need to get on. You ain't got many pages left this side of the bridge."

"Why don't you come with me?" Jack asked. "Think of the adventures we could have, the mischief we could make, the swag we could swipe, the tales people would tell after we passed on through. Jack and the Mostly Good Witch. Why, you could spell us up a flying boat and off we would go."

"You know I can't make flying boats no more, Jack. And besides, I'm a subsidiary character. I've took you as far as I can take you. I've done what I was supposed to do. I give you what I had to give." He pointed at the pail. "And whatever you do—and you listen hard, here, boy—you keep that bucket full of water. You hear me?"

"I will. I promise," Jack said.

"And it will grow wearisome heavy. I am sorry about that."

"I'm still that Jack, somewhat. I'll manage."

The old man grabbed Jack's arm, his witch's grip hard as a hawk-strike. His eyes bleared over with tears, and his chin began to jitter. "Jack..." he began. He swallowed hard and started over. "Jack, if I'd ever had a son of my own, I would've wanted him in some ways to be a little like you."

Jack opened his mouth to thank the old man, and to ask him to let go of his arm, but the old man vanished as suddenly as the sisters in the wheat field, as thoroughly as Tom Dooley into the tempest. He whirled around, slopping a little water out of the bucket as he spun, searching this way and that, but he found that he was alone. "Gotdoggit!" Jack barked. "I'm getting tired of that trick."

Jack found that the clearing had sprouted over with broom sedge and waist-high blackberry briars, and the outbuildings had moldered away. The tree lay on its side, its lone remaining limb beckoning from the bramble like the waving arm of a drowning giant. Only the chimney pile, barely visible in the brush, suggested that a house had ever stood there. Jack choked back a hiccupping sob, his heart iced over with grief. Aside from Mama and his good-for-nothing brothers, the old man had been the first person he had ever known. Sometimes, as he sidled into sleep, it seemed as if there had been another, a somebody else, calling his name, but he was never able to find her.

Just as he stepped onto the forest trail he heard behind him the unmistakable thump of a brick hitting the ground. When he turned he saw, wafting above the toppled chimney, the smoky revenant of an old woman holding a brick over her head. She wound up and heaved another after Jack, although it didn't travel far. He tapped his brow at her in salute. Good, he thought, every fell-down homeplace needed a haint, and a witch haint would be better still. He hoped some lonesome stranger would stray back this way some moonless midnight and she would fright the shit out of him.

Jack eased warily through the woods but no sound reached his hearing save the rush of the flood rising ahead and the bucket chafing against his overall leg and raindrops ticking leaf to leaf on their way down to the forest floor. No giants crashed out of the laurel bellowing their poorly rhymed, Englishman nonsense; no witches stepped into the trail smiling their snaggle-toothed sex smiles, cooing their murderous invitations. The ground was devoid of unicorn sign, and not even a squirrel cast aspersions in his direction. It was disorienting, traveling through a dark forest without running up on something that needed to be outsmarted, diddled, or killed. Waiting for something to happen when it didn't happen proved to be about as scary as the happenings that had.

By the time Jack reached the muddy red road his shoulders were searing from boosting the bucket, and the skin had begun to peel from his palms. He put the water down, cupped his hands, and took a long drink from the pail. What difference could one draught make? He was, after all, toting water to a flood. Jack couldn't yet see the cataracting creek, but the pounding sounded nigh. He stood on the roadside and looked this way and that. Which way was up the lane and which way was down? The old man had told him to follow the muddy red road, but hadn't told him which direction. It was just like a daggum witch to make a riddle out of something as simple as turn left or turn right. And the bridge was as likely to be upstream as it was down.

Then Jack noticed the black dog's tracks headed down the pike (or up, depending) in a rabid path as straight as a plumb line. Each of the prints was as wide as a pie plate, with claw marks long as penknives. His first impulse, of course, was to light out in the opposite direction. Since the black dog was looking for him, going where the dog *wasn't* seemed only intelligent; intuitively, though, he knew that in order for this tale to reach its denouement he had to track it to where it *was.* In the cruelest of conundrums, he had to cross the bridge to get away from the dog, while the bridge was exactly the spot the dog would be. And he had to get to the other side before the flood made the crossing impossible. Jack glanced at the bucket sitting at his feet and briefly considered leaving it behind (typically he never bore any load more burdensome than a bite of dinner), but it was the last thing the old man would ever give him, and worth carrying for no other reason. He hefted it with a wince and set out after the dog.

The road-mud measured ankle-deep and within steps it mounded around Jack's boots into blocks of mire roughly the size of baking-weight possums. His brogans glopped from the muck with sick sucking sounds. The dog tracks filled with seep and looked painted onto the road rather than sunken into it. He rounded each crook expecting to sight the convergence of road, creek, bridge, and dog with which this story was destined to collide, but instead beheld only the next bow in his path.

Just as the torrent's tumult grew so clamorous that Jack's brain began to shout the thoughts inside his head so that he might hear them, the flood bucked into view on his right, walloping wildly through the woods. Young trees caught in the careen slapped at the rising water, while stinking slicks of bank trash sluiced among them. The waves out in the main channel seemed to Jack to rear higher than the ground on which he stood, leaving him with the unsettling impression of looking *up* at the rapid. He could have been facing a giant so seized with fury that no amount of magic truck could've held it at bay. Rather than running away from the giant, however, Jack struggled alongside it. He wrenched one foot at a time free from the ooze, and the bucket banged at his knee. The mud prevented him from quickening this clumping pace, and he watched with rising worry as the water lapped ever closer the road. He hoped the bridge was a high one with mighty timbers and planking cut from ancient trees. A galvanized washtub rode regally atop the rapid as it shot downstream. A pair of raccoon kits clung forlornly to a sweet gum swaying twenty yards out in the current. The body of a yellow cat bobbed in an eddy atop a sodden platter of broom straw and sticks. Jack spewed profane invective at the old man for abandoning him in such a place.

When Jack spied the dog he stepped behind the nearest tree and scouted the situation with the cool eye of a practiced plunderer. It paced stiff-legged before the approach to a narrow wooden bridge that spanned a wide hollow almost topped by the fusillading flood. The dog was behaving strangely, even for a talking beast. Every few feet it stopped pacing, shook each one of its paws, looked back over its shoulder at the heaving creek, and started pacing again.

Across the bridge the muddy red road disappeared into the Yonder woods (which to Jack looked no different from the woods of the settlement) but reappeared in the distance switchbacking up a green hill toward an edifice at the top that

Jack could not identify. The building was one story high and three stories long and seemed to be made out of metal. If it was a castle, it was the strangest one Jack had ever seen. The sight of it, however, inexplicably jolted his heart with joy. He didn't know what the container contained, but was certain that it toted treasure of the rarest kind, the riches he had sought in all his setting out, the hoard he had hoped for all of his days. And it seemed to him, too, in a way he could not explain, that the treasure it held had once been his. But his longing for it made little sense. Jack was not the nostalgic type. To him one kind of boodle was as good as another, and all of it was easier to spend than to shoulder. Yet he knew that if he ever got his hands on the treasure in the metal box he would never let it go; if he ever made it to the top of that hill he would never come down again.

He switched the bucket from his right hand to his left and attempted to form a plan to get himself across the flood unchewed. All he came up with was walking toward the dog hoping that he would think of something along the way. As far as plans went, this one seemed ill-considered, even by Jack's lax standards.

When the dog saw Jack it checked over its shoulder once more, took a few brittle steps toward him, and sat down on its haunches as if it were a good boy. Jack looked again at the white box on the hill and felt the dark rooms inside his chest warming with lamplight. He wiped his nose on his sleeve and started forward; the dog sat still and stared at Jack as he approached. It was even uglier in the daylight than it had been in the dark. Its head was as big as a salt block, but the tiny ears perched atop it looked as if they had been appropriated from a much smaller dog—perhaps one wearing a sweater. Beneath its pounded-flat pug face swung a tongue long enough to outfit two treeing redbones and a yapping fice. Opalescent slings of slobber dangled from its chuffing jowls. Jack stopped twenty yards or so away. The water had risen to roughly a possum tail from the bottom of the bridge.

"Howdy, Daddy," Jack called.

The dog squinted and mouthed, "What?" but Jack couldn't hear its voice over the boom of the flood. He willed himself to move closer and raised his voice.

"I said, 'Speak, boy!' "

The dog growled a spitty laugh. "Your adolescent jabs at humor wound me."

"Good dog!" Jack said.

The dog cocked an ear slightly toward the water boom, took three steps forward, and sat down again.

Jack backed up a corresponding distance and pointed at the far side of the creek with his chin. "Look, Toto, I need to get over there," he said.

"We've been over this bridge business, Jack. Do you want me to latch you now with my rabid bite, or after we watch the creek wash the bridge away?"

"Let me think on that."

"Take your time," the dog said. "The water's risen six inches in the last ten minutes."

"Bingo, I don't have time for this. I have business to tend to in Yonder."

"Oh, please, Jack. I find your delusions almost touching. There's nothing for you in Yonder, as there is nothing for you here. Nobody tells stories anymore. The time of your kind has passed. Let's get this over with."

At that moment, the italicized voice of the old man spoke clearly inside Jack's head: *Jack. Use the bucket.* Jack looked down at the water he had drawn from the old man's well, then grinned up at the dog. Bless you, Old Man, he thought.

"What's in the bucket?" the dog asked.

"It," Jack said.

"What's 'it'?"

"It says not to tell you."

"I'm not stupid," the dog sneered. "Pronouns don't talk."

"You don't say," Jack said.

"That's enough!" snapped the dog. "You go too far with this wordplay." It craned forward and snuffled loudly. "Truly, what's in the bucket? Tell me now or suffer for your reticence." It stood slowly, its hackles high. As it growled a bouquet of slobber and foam bloomed from its nostrils and mouth.

Behind the dog the flood had almost reached the bridge deck.

"Okay, Sparky," Jack said. "You win. It's water."

The dog's spine ridge unhackled. It looked at the bucket, then up at Jack. It backed a step toward the flood. One at a time it lifted and shook its paws. "I don't believe you," it said.

"You usually travel with a bite of dinner but not a drop to drink."

Jack carefully poured a small stream from the bucket onto the ground. "That's water, all right," Jack said. "Cool, clear water. Now I know why you didn't get after us in that rainstorm."

"It's a venomous substance, water," the dog mused. "My burden and my bane. I thirst, yet I cannot drink. I stink, but cannot bathe. It runs as acid through my dreams." The dog lowered itself into a crouch and peeled its lips back over a mammoth array of stalactite teeth.

"Easy there, Lassie," Jack said. "I've got four and a half gallons of water here and I'm not afraid to use it."

"And my mouth is dripping with microbial menace. Put the bucket down, Jack. Slowly."

"No way, Scooby. Step away from the bridge."

The dog stared at Jack and Jack stared at the dog.

"You have no idea how much I want to rip out your trachea and shake it as I would a fat snake," the dog said.

"And I dearly wish that when I threw you off the first bridge you had landed in the creek. What's it gonna be?"

"Okay," the dog said finally. "Victory is yours. My hydrophobia trumps my murderous instincts. Let's circle clockwise until our positions are switched. Then you go your way and I'll go mine."

"Counterclockwise," Jack said for the pleasure of being contentious.

"Fine," the dog snarled.

"How do I know I can trust you?"

"Because I'm a dog."

Jack thought about the assertion for a moment. Dogs were a shit-eating, chicken-killing, leg-humping lot, but in his experience had always been truthful. "That seems about fair," he said.

The dog took a slow step to its right. Jack stepped to his right. The dog took another step and Jack matched it.

When they faced each other halfway through the circle, the dog grinned wickedly. "I hope you can swim," it said.

"I always did hate a talking dog," Jack said. He stepped forward and pitched the bucketful of water into the dog's face.

The dog screamed and flopped to the ground and writhed in the mud and tried to wipe the water out of its eyes with its paws. To Jack's amazement and disgust the skin of its face peeled away as if it were a robber's mask, revealing the marbled bands of gristle binding its great, snapping skull. Its pelt steamed sulfurously and slid from its broad back.

"Jack, you have rendered me!" the dog cried. "We had a deal! Why did you throw water on me?"

"I reckon it's just my nature."

By the time the dog finished melting into a malodorous glop of fur and vitals, the water was running shoe-top high over the bridge deck. The creek hurtled through the hollow in man-tall waves bloodied with red clay; downstream it crashed into the gulch-side and erupted into the laurel in bone-white splays of spray. Only the promise of the treasure in Yonder pulled Jack forward onto the bridge. The water ran smoothly over the planks but with fervid velocity; it grabbed at his boots as he shuffled over the slick boards. He was halfway across when the flood, in a flash, bulged and caught him mid-thigh, stumbling him toward the side of the bridge. A regular man would have been washed off. More frightening, though, was that the bridge—while remaining solid beneath his feet—had disappeared from sight. All around him the brown water thrashed and he imagined himself balanced atop a swaying fence post. He couldn't make himself move another step.

"Help me, Old Man," he begged. "Please help me!"

The voice that answered inside his head wasn't the old man's, but a woman's. He knew the voice better than any other voice, but wasn't able to place it; it belonged to someone he desperately wanted to remember but couldn't quite recall.

"Jack?" the voice said. "Where are you, honey?"

"I'm almost there," he answered, without having any idea where *there* might be.

"Well, hurry on home, then. We're waiting on you."

We, Jack thought. Who's *we? We* was two pages stuck together in a book. And *home? Home* was a dollar gold piece that hit the floor and rolled away. It had to be around here somewhere. "Watch for me," he said.

"All right, then. Bye, Jack."

"Bye."

Jack blinked and found himself still crouching far out in the heave but suddenly he had worked up a crawful of *that* Jack, ax-swinging, giant-killing mad. "No, *sir!*" he shouted at the witch hands of water pulling at him. "Not today. Maybe tomorrow. After a while, but not now." He tightened his grip on the bucket and eased his right foot forward, then moved his left.

He ran out of bridge ten yards before he ran out of creek, but the water had curled into an eddy of only moderate coil and he was able to wade through the chest-high swirl. He refilled his bucket with the silted water and held it over his head as he made the last of his crossing. Once ashore he surprised himself by collapsing onto the muddy red road and weeping like a groom's mother. He cried partly out of gratitude for making it past the black dog and through the flood into Yonder, but mostly in grief at leaving behind the only settlement he had ever known. Had he loved the setting-out skies and dew-tamped roads enough? A bite of dinner by the roadside, a piece of shade in the hot of the day, the sweet waft of wood smoke raveling from a robber's chimney in the cool of an evening. Oh, if only he could pass through it all again!

As Jack sobbed the world grew gradually quiet around him; it finally became so still that he leapt to his feet and spun around as if something were sneaking up on him. Somehow the boom of the flood had receded into the distracted mumbling of an inconspicuous creek in the bottom of an anonymous hollow. A crumbling stone abutment lathered over with poison oak was all that remained of the bridge. Across the creek the green dark wood of white oak and pine and laurel and fern through which he had just passed had been lumberjacked from the settlement, leaving no trace. In its place a rough scrub of briars and alder bushes and twisted Virginia pines scraggled the ridges as far as he could see. You might flush up a rabbit in a waste like that, Jack thought, but you'd never roust out a unicorn. He blew his nose out onto the ground and thought, Well, if I chop on this too long I will surely die. He was where he was and he would go where he would go and it was time to get on with his getting on. He turned away and set off up the muddy red road into Yonder, leaning to his left to balance the bucket he carried on his right, and never once looked back at the settlement.

Jack had traveled no more than a hundred yards up the hill when a familiar-looking black cloud moiled up behind the white treasure box on the summit above him. Surely, surely that anvil-headed son of a bitch hadn't turned around and come back after him. But it inflated at such a precipitous clip that he thought maybe it had. At the first far-off stomps of thunder, Jack gave up on the switchbacks and cut straight up the hillside. The slope was steeper than it had seemed from the road, and the wet grass was slick. The rising cloud was as black as the inside of a box turtle. Jack estimated that the part he could see was already two mountains and a three-headed giant high—and the damn thing was still rising over the hill. He spied that the treasure box had doors and windows, a sight that heartened him. Maybe the door wasn't locked, or didn't require magic spell-words to get it open. Did magic spell-words even work in Yonder?

He had nearly reached the top of the hill—the treasure house was within a rock throw—when an unfamiliar oppression of tiredness settled on him. He set the bucket down to catch his breath. The coming cloud roiled like boiling blackstrap. Lizard flicks of lightning snapped at the far side of the hill, followed almost immediately by rifled rips of thunder. When he reached again for the bucket bail the words *window unit* cleaved his skull with such force that he dropped straight to the ground, where he moaned and wept and scraped at the dirt with his heels and clutched at his head, afraid that brain-slop was sludging from his ear-holes. Window unit? he thought. What the hell is a window unit? But then he was standing on a chair in front of an icy blast of air, looking at numbers. When I turn it toward one it gets hotter, and when I turn it toward ten it gets colder. Onetwothreefourfivesixseveneightnineten. Tennineeightsevensixfivefourthreetwoone. He turned it back to ten and pulled up his shirt and pressed his belly against the air holes. It must have snow in there. Mama said, Jack, you get down from there and stop messing with that thing before you break it.

Window unit.

And then other strange words hacked into his brain—*Microwave Fanny pack Labradoodle*—and rushed into the widening cleft—*Doublewide Nacho Chainsaw*—until the accumulating knowledge of a regular man named John, known since childhood as Jack, began to exceed the ability of *that* Jack to comprehend. And the words which *that* Jack had known best—*New ground Hardhead Unicorn*—mounted a slow retreat into the deepest ganglia of his mind, where they cried out in a fading whisper.

When Jack opened his eyes, the black cloud churned over him as if trying to figure out whether or not he was still alive, as if to say, If you *are* still alive I will suck the breath out of you soon enough. He rolled over onto his hands and knees, still drunk on fresh words, and stumbled to his feet. New words still tippled into his skull pan—*Pep rally Wide receiver Pepperoni Bra hook*—but they stung less and less. He squinted at the white box until it came back into focus. That was his house. And it was a double-wide! By God, he lived in a double-wide! It was wider than wide! Better than good! *Fellowship hall Fruit punch Pensacola Trojan.* And he was married! He was married and he lived with his wife in a house that was better than good because it was wider than wide! He grabbed up the bucket and staggered forward.

He had almost made it to the yard when he pulled up short and set the bucket on the ground. Well, shit. He couldn't think of his wife's name. He put his hands on his hips and closed his eyes and turned slowly in a circle. Think, Jack, think. She's the only girl you've ever loved! You took baths together as babies and she cried when you peed in the water. You gave her a mood ring in the fifth grade. *Hickey Humvee Polyester Snooze button.* Susan? Don't think so. *Double play Toaster oven Breast pump Tilt-a-Whirl.* Uhura? Nope. What did he call her when he told her good night? What if she didn't even have a name? *Yosemite Pesto Goldfish Bass boat.* Daggummit, he hoped she'd be wearing a *Name tag.*

The black cloud had grown so tall that Jack could no longer see its top. It dropped a sniffing hound's snout from its trailing edge. Uh-oh, that wasn't good. Jack caught up the bucket with the creek water and hurried through the yard. He jumped onto the small porch and jerked open the door. It was dark inside. The first thing he saw was a bald man wearing suspenders talking inside a picture frame on the wall. A witch must have sneaked into the treasure house, but what kind of witch lived in a picture frame?

Then he saw her. Jill! Sweet Lord, how could he have forgotten Jill? *Jill Jill Jill.* That one word would be a fair trade for all the other words he'd ever known, or would know. After he'd lost her he had searched for her for so long he'd forgotten what he was looking for. All that setting out. It felt as if he'd been looking for her for centuries, but how could that be?

When Jill saw him a web of worry lifted from her face. "Jack, honey, where have you been?" She pointed at the bald man talking in the picture frame. "The weatherman says the radar's got a hook echo on it."

He held up the bucket. "I fetched you a pail of water," he said.

She blinked at him and he saw in her face that—just for a troubling second—a shade of the old settlement had spirited past her recalling. "Oh, Jack, that is so sweet. But come look at this."

The bald witch in the picture pointed at some kind of map covered with what looked like a curdle of blood coiling and uncoiling over top of it. Nothing Jack saw made any sense to him. Why was there blood on the bald witch's map? Why was everything in the picture *moving?* He set the bucket on the floor and stepped over to the window. Beneath the cloud snout a thin twist of something like smoke helixed upward from the ground. The helix spun into a writhe of black dirt that braided into the cloud's sucking maw. A rapid of rain blasted against the double-wide's side and everything beyond disappeared save for the beating water itself. The house wobbled and strained against its anchors. Well, Jack thought. It's run us to ground.

He turned toward Jill just as she stood and faced him. *Sonic screwdriver The quicker picker upper Everything must go.* "Jill!" he yelled. "We need to get to our place of safety!"

He saw her sob, and the sight rent his chest with the force of a broadax lopping off a giant's head.

"Oh, Jack," she wailed, "we don't *have* a place of safety."

Jack opened his mouth to speak but found that the only words he knew were useless ones. *All you can eat shrimp.* How do you say I have loved you since we first went up the hill lo those many years ago? That I will love you until the end of the last story? No word he could utter would ever reflect the degree to which he meant it. He stepped toward her and shook his head and raised his palms helplessly at his sides.

"I've got to get Little Jack!" she screamed.

Jack felt as if a catamount had clawed out his heart. He went swimmy-headed. Little Jack. By God, there *was* a Little Jack.

Little Jack Little Jack Little Jack.

"No, wait!" he yelled. "Let me get him!"

But before he could take a step toward the hallway the

sofa rose from the carpet and whirled onto its end and the window frames twisted from their sockets and lifted off into the darkness. Jill's feet flew from beneath her and she flailed into the air and ripped splayed through the ceiling. The walls of the house lifted from around Jack and the storm jerked him into the howling black. Wild beasts fanged him about the face while he flew and unicorns horned him through the tripes; cuckolded robbers sliced his sinews loose from his bones and a giant sundered his skull bone with a cudgel. He found no joy in the flying and only screaming fear in the falling. And then he lay flat on his back in a field watching pink snow fall from the sky. A flock of blank paper lit gingerly on the ground around him. He listened for Jill to call his name, for Little Jack to cry to be found, but the world was as quiet as a flyleaf. He felt every word he had ever known leaking from his busted crown and he knew that soon he wouldn't know any words at all.

Not quite regular man and not quite *that* Jack, he lay still and considered his condition with the language he had left. The word *death* meant death, of course, and it meant nothing at all. All it said was, there's the door, Jack, you get on now, and what good is a word like that? It said nothing about whatever came next. Jack shook with amazement. He had never before set foot in a story with an honest-to-goodness conclusion. He had lived in one continuous tale. All of his life, one page had turned after another and he had set out down another road—looking, he finally remembered, for Jill. But now he understood that every second of joy in the life of a regular man bloomed from the spreading blight of his dying. And he wasn't ready to leave the page. He had only just set down here, into this brilliant world of numbered mornings, into the finespun possibility of human joy. He wanted to teach Little Jack to play baseball because he had only just learned about it himself. He wanted to brush with his finger the first tress of silver to light up in Jill's dark hair. He wanted to sit with her on the porch in the bug-chanting twilight and share a cold, sweating beer. He wanted to make pancakes on Sunday morning. He wanted to live as a regular man until his ancient heart said, old friend, I can't beat no more. Then he wanted to kiss Jill's hand and laugh out loud because he had chewed every last bit of sweet out of the regular life he had been given. Jack raised his arms toward the tin-colored sky and earnestly spoke to whoever might be listening. "The book," he whispered. "For God's sake, don't close this book."

About the Author

Tony Earley is the author of the novels *Jim the Boy* and *The Blue Star.* His fiction has earned a National Magazine Award and appeared in *The New Yorker, Harper's, Esquire,* and *The Best American Short Stories.* Earley was chosen for both *The New Yorker*'s inaugural best 20 Under 40 list of fiction writers and *Granta*'s 20 Best Young American Novelists. He lives with his family in Nashville, Tennessee, where he is the Samuel Milton Fleming Professor of English at Vanderbilt University.